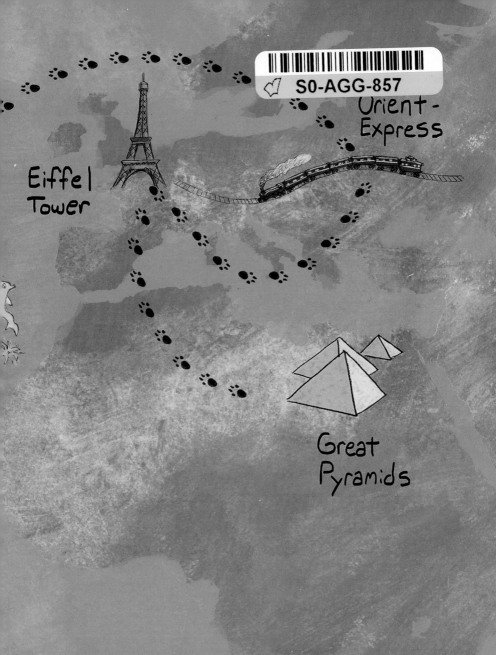

Eiffel
Tower

Orient-
Express

Great
Pyramids

a Snoutz adventure

SNOUTZ

Pipper's
Secret
Ingredient

Kathryn —
at the end of the
day, it's all
about love —
xxx Jane

a Snoutz adventure

Pipper's Secret Ingredient

SNOUTZ

by Jane Murphy and Allison Fingerhuth

illustrations by Neal Sharp

Mutt Media

New York

a Snoutz adventure
Published by Mutt Media
April 2012

Mutt Media
225 East 74th Street | Suite 3H
New York, NY 10021

ISBN 10: 0-6153880-8-6
ISBN 13: 978-0-615-38808-3

Printed in the United States of America

The Library of Congress has cataloged the hardcopy format(s) as follows:
Library of Congress Control Number: 2010910689
Pipper's Secret Ingredient | Jane Murphy and Allison Fingerhuth

Book design and production by Sara De Pasquale Ortmanns
welcome@d.signconsultant.ch | www.d.signconsultant.ch ®

For Lu, Zoe, Ruby and Marbles – our Snoutz family – who travel the world with their own senses of adventure and tastebuds. And extra hugs to Beat and Jerry for their support and love of all things Snoutz.

Contents

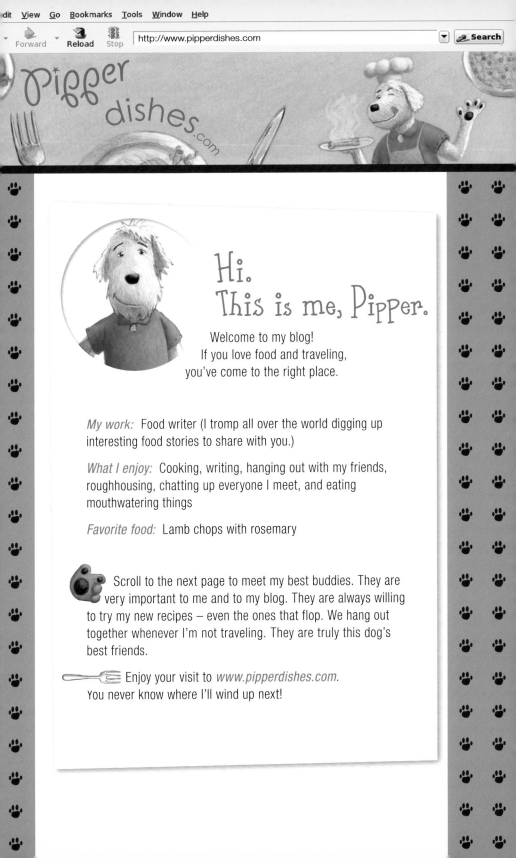

Hi.
This is me, Pipper.

Welcome to my blog!
If you love food and traveling,
you've come to the right place.

My work: Food writer (I tromp all over the world digging up interesting food stories to share with you.)

What I enjoy: Cooking, writing, hanging out with my friends, roughhousing, chatting up everyone I meet, and eating mouthwatering things

Favorite food: Lamb chops with rosemary

Scroll to the next page to meet my best buddies. They are very important to me and to my blog. They are always willing to try my new recipes – even the ones that flop. We hang out together whenever I'm not traveling. They are truly this dog's best friends.

Enjoy your visit to *www.pipperdishes.com*.
You never know where I'll wind up next!

Hilda

Her work: Firefighter (and daredevil)

What she enjoys: Roller coasters, motorcycles, and rescuing cats from trees

Favorite food: Her Five-alarm Chili

Sophie

Her work: Librarian (She reads more than anyone I know.)

What she enjoys: Learning things, playing poker, and reading my blog

Favorite food: Alphabet soup (She makes up new words as she slurps.)

Archibald

His work: Designer/inventor (He invents cool things to make life easier. Do you have a never-empty water bowl, too?)

What he enjoys: Taking things apart and putting them back together in new ways, chasing squirrels, visiting the design museum, and hunting for antiques

Favorite food: His Uncle Nigel's Pork Pie

Sydney

His work: Mail carrier (and wannabe rock star)

What he enjoys: Going to rock festivals, playing air guitar, and talking to everyone on his route

Favorite food: My Very Blueberry Ice Cream

Chance

His work: Personal trainer (and professional worrywart)

What he enjoys: Eating healthy, keeping fit, and watching The Weather Channel

Favorite food: Cucumber sandwiches (on pumpernickel bread)

Pipper Puzzles Over Her Next Food Story

It was midnight in Fetchwood. A stray cat, wandering through town, gazed at the silvery sliver of the moon in the night sky. Meanwhile, Pipper was tossing and turning. She rolled over and rolled back. She fluffed up her pillow and tugged at the blanket. Then she felt hot and tossed off the blanket. She simply couldn't sleep. You probably know what that's like. Anyway, she decided she might as well get up and get some work done.

Pipper sat down at her desk and stared at her computer. This popular world-roving, bowl-sniffing, recipe-tasting blogger was clueless. Where should she go? What would she write about? It was the first time ever that Pipper had a problem coming up with an idea. It was like trying to decide what to get your best friend for her birthday when nothing seems just right.

Pipper has nosed all around the globe to visit food festivals and farms, cook-offs and restaurant openings. She loves blogging all about her experiences for her loyal readers. Her room is filled with memories. You'd be impressed for sure. She looked at the things on her wall and thought back on all the fun she'd had over the years. There was a picture of her stuck in a pickle barrel at the International Pickle Fest.Hanging nearby was her certificate for lifting the world's biggest bagel at the Bagel Bash in Syracuse.

Pipper's twitching nose meant she was thinking hard. She thought to herself, *I'm stumped. I've never run out of ideas before. Hmmm. Maybe this one will do.* She began to type…

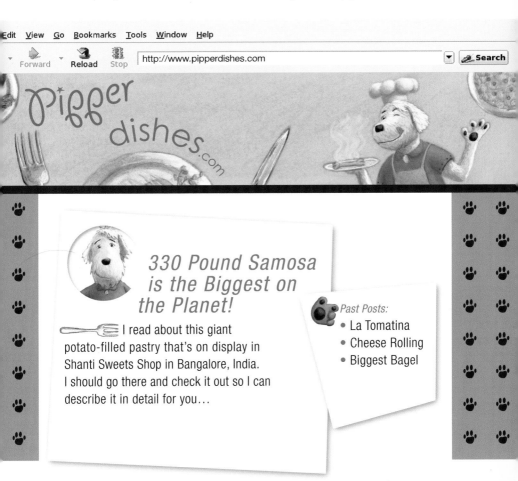

Edit View Go Bookmarks Tools Window Help

Forward   Reload   Stop   http://www.pipperdishes.com   Search

Pipper dishes.com

330 Pound Samosa is the Biggest on the Planet!

I read about this giant potato-filled pastry that's on display in Shanti Sweets Shop in Bangalore, India. I should go there and check it out so I can describe it in detail for you…

Past Posts:
* La Tomatina
* Cheese Rolling
* Biggest Bagel

Oh, forget that idea. It's too far to go for a bite of a Samosa. I can just walk over to Patel's Tandoori across town and munch on one. Or, I could make my own. Let's see, how's this idea?

Pipper dishes.com

Eat Your Paper!

My friend Pete in Chicago wrote me about a chef there who is experimenting with food ideas. His latest invention is flavored paper. Apparently, he has one that tastes like cheesecake…

Past Posts:
- La Tomatina
- Cheese Rolling
- Biggest Bagel

Today's Recipe:
Sesame-topped Samosas

Pipper considered to herself, *I could interview him and see what else he's created. Maybe…Nah, that's a no-drooler. Who cares about eating cheesecake-flavored paper when you can eat the real thing. I need to dig up something different – a real* **BOW WOW** *… Hmmm, I'm tired from all this thinking. Guess I'll turn on the TV and relax a bit.*

Pipper switched on the remote and surfed to Larry King Spaniel's talk show. Usually, she couldn't stay awake late enough to watch it. Larry was introducing his guest.

"We're back with Bull Bogus, president of the Bogus Biscuit Company. So, Bull, what do you have to say about your biscuits making your customers sick, causing allergies, and fattening bellies?"

"Why Larry, that's a pile of dirty kitty litter. My family's been making biscuits for more than twenty-five years," Bogus sputtered, sending bits of slobber towards Larry.

"Yes, you took over the company two years ago, after your father retired," Larry said. "Back then, Bogus Biscuits were number one. Why wouldn't you want to follow your father's paw prints?" he asked his guest.

Pipper sat, curled up in her pajamas, in front of the TV watching Bogus squirm on camera.

"We needed to cut costs and increase profits," Bogus blabbered. "So we developed a cheaper, uh, I mean, better way to make the same top-notch biscuits." His eyes darted back and forth nervously.

Pipper listened intently as Larry continued to hound Bogus. "Your father must have been doing something right. Before you took over, sales were strong and nobody complained of rashes or bellyaches. These days, many believe that your biscuits are made of nothing but chemicals."

"Malarkey! We're still making real biscuits," Bogus insisted, with a growl.

"Grumbles are coming from across the nation, Bull," Larry reported. "They are saying that you're no longer living up to your advertising claim 'It's not a real biscuit, unless it's Bogus.'"

"That's still our claim, and we're sticking to it," Bogus insisted as he licked some drool from the side of his jowls.

"Our callers have questions for you, too, Bull. Rinaldo from Rochester, you're on the line," Larry welcomed.

"Hi, Larry. Thanks for taking my call. Mr. Bogus, I've read your sales are down and your business investors are getting worried. They are thinking of taking back the money they put in the company. Either that, or they plan to kick you out the door. What do you have to say?" Rinaldo asked.

"We're working on something new and unique that will put Bogus Biscuits back on top," Bull declared as a large drop of spittle landed on Larry's nose.

Larry pried, "I heard you're running out of time. When can the public and your investors expect these new biscuits?"

"By the end of the month," Bogus shot back.

Larry took the next caller. "Stella from San Bernadino, you're on the line."

"Hi, Larry. I'm curious, Mr. Bogus, can you give us a hint what this new biscuit will be like?" Stella asked.

"Uh, well, I don't want to give anything away. Let's just say, it'll make your tail spin," Bogus laughed as he slapped his paw on Larry's desk.

"Good luck to that guy," Pipper said. Then she yawned and turned off her TV.

She was finally feeling sleepy. She figured she should snooze a bit before it was really time to wake and shake. Her friends were coming for sushi that night. In just a few hours, she would have to get up and go shopping. She crawled back under the covers and started dreaming about her friends.

In her first dream, she was at the library with Sophie who kept bringing her piles of travel books. Then Pipper was doing yoga at the gym with Chance. While they were each in the lotus position, he reminded her to create a list of ideas for future blogs. He also told her to check The Weather Channel to be sure to avoid rainy spots.

That's Chance. He is always watching out and being careful. He even looks both ways, twice, before crossing the street, she thought in her sleep.

Pipper's ears flapped on her pillow as she continued dreaming.

Next, she was with Sidney on his mail route, helping him deliver letters and packages. She tried to get him to suggest ideas for her next story. But, Sidney was so into listening to a new song on his earphones, he didn't hear her.

Aren't dreams weird? You're in your bed, but you're also in your dream. There was Pipper on her back, paws shaking in the air, as Sidney disappeared from her thoughts.

Now, she saw herself running to meet Archibald who gave her his newest invention: a raincoat that transformed into a carry-on bag. Ingenious! Pipper told him she loved it but explained she didn't know her next destination.

Then Pipper dreamed she was with Hilda at the firehouse, eating Hilda's famous chili. She confessed to being baffled about her next blog. Suddenly, the fire alarm sounded. Pipper woke up. The fire alarm was actually her alarm clock ringing. The sun was up, and it was time for Pipper to be up, too.

Pipper's Big Idea

That whole day, Pipper tried to come up with a new food story. She pondered over this at the fish store. She sighed about it at the flower shop. She even moaned about it, sitting with her bundles on the bus home.

Suddenly, she noticed a Bogus Biscuit Company billboard sign floating past the bus window. She chuckled at their motto: "It's not a real biscuit, unless it's Bogus!" Pipper thought, *It's not a real biscuit, if it* is *Bogus!*

The day flew by. Pipper didn't have a chance to return to her computer. She still didn't have a clue what to write about anyway.

That evening, everyone was in the kitchen helping Pipper put out the dinner fixings. Archibald and Hilda wolfed down a few sushi rolls from the serving platter. "These tuna and avocado rolls are doggone delicious."

Hilda agreed with Archibald. "I hope there will be leftovers to take back to the firehouse."

"Thanks guys. At least something is going right today," Pipper admitted.

Hilda reached for the dipping sauce and gazed at her friend. "What's the matter, Pipp?"

Pipper wrinkled up her nose and frowned. "I tossed and turned all night trying to think of something interesting for my next food story. My imagination is drier than my uncle Leo's turkey burgers. Nothing seems that exciting. Or if it does, I realize I've already written about it."

Sidney was concerned that Pipper was not her frisky self. "You just need to get back in your groove. I have just the thing to help you – the new Crunchy Bones CD, *Teeth*." Sidney pulled a CD from the back pocket of his uniform pants. He slipped the disk in the player, and did his paw-pumping Sidney strut over to the table.

Archibald opened the Expanda Chopsticks he designed and reached for a salmon and cucumber roll. "Honestly,

Pipper, I never thought you would run out of ideas. Your mind has been going since we were pups."

Hilda chimed in, "You might get a boost riding on my new Street Rover bike. It always clears my mind when the wind blows through my fur, and I catch bugs in my teeth."

"I don't know about that, but this book looks very useful." Sophie held up a copy of *Jams, Pickles, and Hot Water: a guide for travelers who find themselves in unusual situations*. "We'll help you think of something," she encouraged Pipper.

"We absolutely have to," Hilda insisted. "I look forward to your blog posts as much as I look forward to putting out fires. I loved how you got rained on with tomatoes at the La Tomatina Festival in Spain. Ninety thousand pounds of tossed tomatoes sounded pretty thrilling – and pretty messy."

"My fur was red for a week," Pipper said, smiling. "Cleaning up was harder than my hose-down at the world pizza championship. Remember, I walked past a man tossing his pie and it landed on my head? I smelled pretty garlicky. But this time – I don't know. I'm just frustrated."

While Sidney panted at the treats, he proposed, "If we put our noses together, we'll sniff out a super idea for you."

"This time, I want to take on something more challenging than lifting bagels and carving radishes," Pipper insisted. "I need to find something I can really sink my teeth into."

As the plate of mussel delights crossed by Chance's nose he piped up, "Well, I'm not sinking my teeth into those.

I heard they make you turn green if they're not fresh. I'll pass, thank you very much. You know, I always say, better safe than sorry."

"They're fresh from the sea. Come on. Take a chance, Chance," Hilda teased.

"It's true. I took a leap eating Hilda's wasabi biscuits," Archibald confessed. "They are scrumptious, but they can set off five-alarm gas explosions. After those spicy treats, I had to invent a whole new deep-penetrating air freshener. I could barely stand myself."

"Finding a healthy treat that everyone likes is as tough as finding a book everyone likes. There are so many different tastes," Sophie mused, grabbing the last salmon roll. "Everyone is into something different. Of course, I don't know anyone who is into Bogus Biscuits."

"I tried their Boffo Banana Biscuits and wound up with a stomach ache for a week," Archibald complained. "Their weird shapes didn't even look like bananas. Bad design, if you ask me."

Hilda added, "Once, I had a Bogus Flame Starter biscuit. It felt like there were flames in my stomach. I like spicy food. But that was over the top. I had to drink gallons of water to put out that fire."

"I saw Bull Bogus on TV late last night when I couldn't sleep. Larry King Spaniel grilled him about the chemicals and high fat in his recipes. He asked Bogus about allergies and other bad reactions to his biscuits. Bogus growled that all that talk was just whimpering nonsense. Then he announced that his food scientists are working on a new formula that will be their best ever."

"I bet they wouldn't know a good ingredient if it bit them in the tail," Chance insisted. "When it comes to treats, it's got to be good for our insides and outsides. Vitamins and minerals are what matter."

"I think a treat should look good. If it has a cool design, I'll try it," Archibald proclaimed.

Hilda swiveled on her stool and dizzily clamored, "Oh come on, a good treat should be something fun and exciting. When I bite into it, I want to think to myself *BAD DOG*."

Sidney jumped in. "I think a treat should be a delicious reward for doing something well. You know, like singing on key."

"You could be right, Sidney. After all, it is like dessert. You wouldn't eat dessert before your vegetables."

"I might, Sophie," Sidney quibbled. "Remember that song, 'Bonbons for Breakfast' by the Sweet Peas?"

"You have a song for every situation, Sidney," Hilda chuckled.

Sophie politely raised her paw so as not to interrupt. "Perhaps there's something we haven't even thought of that makes a treat perfect."

"I've got it!" Pipper yipped. Everyone looked up in surprise.

"What are you talking about, Dog?" Sidney asked.

"You're all arguing about what makes the perfect treat. That's it. That's what I am going to write about – the secret ingredient for a perfect treat. Besides, all this yapping over the Bogus Biscuit Company got me thinking. Why couldn't there be an ingredient that's good for everyone? No more tummyaches, allergies, and overweight bellies hitting the ground when we walk. There must be something out there, perhaps some long-lost secret ingredient."

All her friends gathered around Pipper. They were curious about what she was suggesting. Hilda's left eyebrow went up, "You think that's exciting?"

"It is," Pipper replied. "Don't you see? You each believe something different about what makes a treat special. Archibald thinks it's what it looks like. Chance thinks it has to be healthy. Hilda thinks it should be fun. Sidney's take is that it's a delicious reward. And Sophie, you just might be right. It could be something totally unexpected. My quest is to discover which of these things rules."

"A quest?" Hilda shouted.

"Yes," Pipper confirmed. "I am going in search of the secret to the perfect treat. Is it the design? The healthfulness? The thrill? The award-winning yumminess? Or is it something else?"

"Brilliant," Sophie exclaimed.

"Model idea," Archibald enthused.

"Thrilling," Hilda yelped.

"Knockout hit," Sidney trilled.

"Are you sure?" Chance puzzled.

"I'm sure," Pipper said confidently. "But first, I have to plan my trip."

Everyone chipped in with ideas for where Pipper should go and experts she could interview. After some discussion, she went online and made her reservations.

The first stop on her journey was Cairo, Egypt, to visit the Great Pyramid of Giza. Archibald begged her to check it out. He believed it might reveal a clue to great design. After all, he was head over tail about genius construction. He arranged for a special guide, Mr. Saluki, to meet her at the airport.

All Pipper had left to do was pack her backpack.

Pipper dishes.com

Taking Off!

This is just a quick update to let you, my loyal readers, know I'm off on my next food adventure.

The other night, I was sitting around with my pack of friends, eating sushi. We got to chatting about the allergies, tummyaches, and extra fat caused by many treats on the market. Also, everybody has such different taste.

We just couldn't agree on what makes a perfect treat. So, I'm on a hunt to find the secret ingredient to the perfect treat.

My first stop is Cairo, Egypt, and the Great Pyramid of Giza. I will be blogging as I go. So, stay in touch.

Past Posts:
- Ice Sculptures to Melt Your Heart
- Jell-O Museum Exhibit Shakes Things Up

Today's Recipe:
Seven Grain Buns for the Road

Bark Back…
Safe travels and good luck on your search. Can't wait to read all about it.

Miles Maltese
(Miami, Florida)

Bull Bogus Has Plans of His Own

Over the next few weeks, Pipper would be flying the skies, riding the rails, squeezing on a subway, hiking, and biking to five different destinations. (Check out the inside cover map and see the route she will follow in her search for the secret ingredient.) Her plans were set. She had all her tickets. Little did she know that Bull Bogus had plans of *his* own.

In fact, at the very moment Pipper's plane started flying, Bull Bogus was flying into a rage. He wanted the new biscuits to be on sale by the end of the month. And it didn't look like it was going to happen. He hounded his food scientists to come up with the formula. What a bully!

"Mitzi!" Bogus barked at his head researcher as he walked into the test kitchen.

"Yes, Mr. B, sir."

"Did you see me on the Larry King Spaniel show?" he asked loudly.

"I did, Mr. B," Mitzi replied.

"Well, how did I look, Mitzi?" Bogus prodded. "Could you see my double chin?"

"No, Mr. B. You looked great, sir. Really great," Mitzi

fibbed, as she looked up at all his chins.

"Good. Tell me, Mitzi, do you read the Pipper Dishes blog?"

"Yes, Mr. B, sir," Mitzi replied enthusiastically. "I absolutely lap up those food adventures of hers."

"Well, what's all this about a secret ingredient?" Bogus spat.

"I don't know, Mr. B, sir," Mitzi answered meekly.

"Well, why the ham hocks not?" Bogus bellowed. "If anybody is going to get that secret ingredient, it's going to be me! I promised our investors a new formula by the end of the month. Now you get back to work. None of this good for you organic stuff, and no fancy gourmet treats. I think all that is just balderdash. Start whipping up something we can sell. I'll see about getting our paws on this secret ingredient."

As Bogus started to leave, Mitzi shook nervously and asked, "How will you get the secret ingredient, sir? Is there some way I can help?"

"No. I've got that covered." Bogus turned back to face her and declared, "Your work is here in the test kitchen, Mitzi."

Then he pounced back to his office and shuffled through some papers. Within moments, he pressed the button on his intercom and said, "Ms. Windhound, get me Bumbles Brug on the phone."

Mitzi padded quietly over to Bogus' thick office door and tried to listen. All she heard were snippets of Bogus talking. "…job for you…secret…Come tomorrow."

Mitzi became flustered and paced the hallway on her tiny paws. "Oh, dear, oh, dear. What is Mr. B up to now? Whatever it is, it can't be good." She continued pacing back and forth. "What shall I do? What shall I do? OK, think! Air. I need to get some air." Mitzi hightailed it out of the building. Just as she pushed open the door, she collided with Sidney who was dancing along with his mailbag. Everything in his bag spilled to the ground.

"Oh, I'm so sorry." Mitzi helped Sidney pick up his things. She realized she knew that face. "You're Sidney, aren't you? I recognize you from the Pipper blog. What a coincidence running into you. I was just talking about Pipper with my boss."

"Pipper gets lots of folks talking," Sidney replied.

"I don't have much time. I have to get back before Mr. Bogus catches me." Mitzi looked around her and said almost in a whisper. "I think your friend, Pipper, might be in some trouble."

Sidney's eyebrows went up. "What are you talking about? Pipper just left on a plane to Egypt."

"I know. Bogus read all about her trip.

He wants to get his paws on the secret ingredient. I think he is hiring someone to get it from her. Pipper may be in danger. Unfortunately, my boss is capable of a lot of things. And most of them aren't good."

"You must be eating some crazy Bogus Biscuits," Sidney remarked in disbelief.

"Please trust me. I must get back. Maybe we can meet later, and I'll tell you everything," Mitzi quivered.

Sidney put two and two together. First of all, Bogus promised his investors and his customers a new biscuit. Second, Pipper was tracking down a secret ingredient for the perfect treat. No wonder he wanted her followed. Sidney was convinced Mitzi's concern must be for real. "I'll do anything for Pipper. She's my best friend."

Sidney started to worry and wanted to hear more about what Mitzi had learned. He had to get back to work, so he suggested she meet everyone at Pipper's place. They were going over to water the plants and feed the fish. They always did that whenever Pipper was traveling. He scribbled the address on the back of some junk mail and asked her to show up at six o'clock.

Mitzi grabbed the address and ran back inside. Sidney didn't hesitate and sent a text message to Pipper.

B careful. some1 wrkin 4 the Bogus Biscuit Co may b folwin u. He culd b dangerous. They may wnt 2 find the secret ingredient 2. XO, Sidney

File   Edit   View   Go   Bookmarks   Tools   Window   Help

Back   Forward   Reload   Stop   http://www.pipperdishes.com   Se

Pipper dishes.com

Arriving in Egypt

The captain just announced it's a paw-sweaty 96°F (36°C) afternoon at Cairo International Airport.

"Ahlan wa sahlan" – that's how they say *"welcome"* in Egypt.

The Great Pyramid of Giza is one of the Seven Wonders of the Ancient World. Archibald was panting with excitement about me coming here. You'd have thought he was going with Mr. Saluki himself.

I thought I should be prepared. So, I've been digging through a book Sophie gave me about Egyptian history. Chew on this... Bread was a big deal thousands of years ago in the time of the pharaohs. There were cat- and bird-shaped breads made to please the gods. Wouldn't the gods have liked some dog-shaped breads too?

All this bread talk is making me hungry. I could eat another Seven Grain Bun. Uh-oh, my seat is filled with crumbs from the one I already scarfed down. ☺

We're landing soon. Guess I'll shut down my computer.

Salam alekum *(peace be upon you).*

Past Posts:
- The Real Eel
- Garlic to the Rescue
- Rolling Sushi

Today's Recipe:
Sushi with Wasabi Biscuits and Soy Dipping Sauce
(It's a real .)

Bark Back...
Rolled some sushi for the ladies last night. Rice stuck in my paws. Be sure to wear gloves!

Florence Flanders
(Toledo, Ohio)

At the Great Pyramid of Giza

Pipper entered the noisy and crowded Cairo airport. She was groggy after her long flight. Other travelers jostled her as they hurried past on their way to and from their planes. Suddenly, she spotted a sign that said PIPPER in big orange letters. She waved and approached the hound holding the sign, pointing at herself.

"Ahlan wa sahlan (welcome), my honored guest. I am Mr. Saluki, your guide to our greatest pyramid. It is a pleasure to have you here in my country. Archibald wrote me all about you."

Mr. Saluki led Pipper to his Jeep. "May I offer you a chewy Chickpea Pomegranate Biscuit and some cool mint tea? You must need to eat something after such a long journey."

"Thanks. I'm starving. Do you think we have time for a kebab?"

"Sorry, we have no time for kebabs. Archibald planned a full trip for you. So, hop in and buckle up. We'll have lunch when we get to Giza."

Mr. Saluki stepped on the gas pedal, and the Jeep jerked forward. They headed into the clogged streets of Cairo. Everyone kept changing lanes. Mr. Saluki moved to the right, ahead of a guy in a pickup truck filled with flat tires.

Then a honking taxi pulled in front of them. Pipper tilted on the seat with every swerve as they passed narrow streets and open markets. The traffic was stop-and-go all along the curving green Nile River.

They were forced to come to a halt for a horse-drawn taxi making a U-turn. Then they made their way out of the city's buzz. Pipper looked back at all the minarets rising from the rooftops of the city's mosques. She remembered reading in one of Sophie's books that Cairo is nicknamed the "City of a Thousand Minarets." Pipper thought they looked like a thousand lighthouses. She admired the view until they arrived in the desert.

"Hang on, Pipper," Mr. Saluki said as he changed gears on the Jeep.

"Whoaaa," Pipper squealed as she fell back in her seat. They tackled the sand dunes at full speed. Her hair swirled, and her cheeks flapped as they shot up and skidded down. "This is better than the Looney Looper at Gut Churn Park."

Mr. Saluki laughed. "It's almost as fun as some camel rides I've had." After they bounced and bumped a few more times over the sand hills, Mr. Saluki brought the Jeep to a stop. They arrived at a brilliant red tent in the Western desert. Two camels were waiting outside. They wouldn't have fit in the tent. Besides, what would a camel do in a tent?

"These are my desert companions, Lumpy I and Lumpy II."

Pipper looked up. "They sure are tall." She followed Mr. Saluki cautiously as he approached the camels.

"Camels are expert travelers. They can go for weeks without food or water. Lumpy I and Lumpy II can save food in their humps for when they need it." Mr. Saluki patted Lumpy I on his hump. "They're also calm in troubling situations."

Pipper wondered what Mr. Saluki meant by "troubling situations."

"*Koosh*," commanded Mr. Saluki. The camels gently knelt down. "OK, Pipper, hop on, and we'll take off."

"*Hut-hut*." The camels obeyed Mr. Saluki's command. They stood up and started walking as Mr. Saluki began the next part of his tour.

"My Egyptian family goes back a long time. Salukis were here more than four thousand years ago when the pyramids were being built. Imagine! It took thousands of workers to construct these giant tombs. Everything was carried in carts and by paw. There weren't any trucks or cars back then."

They traveled on. Pipper looked out over the desert. She tried to imagine what it was like with thousands of workers trudging through the sand. She wondered how they worked in the sizzling sun. She especially wondered what they had to eat. Mr. Saluki must have guessed what she was thinking.

"One of my ancestors, great-great-great-great-great (add one hundred more greats) Grandaunt Safi was famous for her koftas. She would bring piles of these tasty meatballs to the pyramid builders for lunch. In fact, there is a painting of her on a wall in one of the pyramids. She is balancing a meatball in each paw."

Mr. Saluki and Pipper became distracted as Lumpy II began madly sniffing the air. Pipper had no idea what Lumpy II was up to. Mr. Saluki, who seemed amused by the sniffing camel, alerted Pipper. "Uh-oh, he smells dates."

"Dates?" asked Pipper.

"He's crazy about them, pits and all." Pipper gasped as Lumpy II bolted forward.

"Hold on, Pipper," Mr. Saluki called after her. Pipper shut her eyes and wrapped herself around Lumpy II's hump. When she finally peeked around her, she noticed other camels with their riders running beside them. Pipper hadn't realized that they had joined a camel race, and Lumpy II was in the lead. He shot across the finish line and gobbled up a bunch of dates that were piled next to the trophy.

A crowd waiting at the finish line whooped and cheered. Everyone praised the unknown rider. Pipper was flustered as she accepted the sandstone crown trophy. "I should have warned you about the dates," Mr. Saluki confessed as he and Lumpy I sauntered up to Pipper. "Lumpy II can't resist their sweetness."

"Hopefully, we won't ride past any date trees," Pipper laughed. As she placed the winner's trophy in Lumpy II's saddlebag, she glimpsed him smiling with his date-filled belly.

"It's a good thing that race wasn't long. We only lost a little time and didn't go too far off our route. Let's continue our journey, and I'll tell you about Granduncle Ebo. He was an amazing camel rider who could balance himself standing

up on the hump of his camel. He got invited to perform at many celebrations and festivals in the desert."

Mr. Saluki sure had lots of stories to tell. He was chatting away about his granduncle when, suddenly, he stopped talking and stared into the distance. Pipper followed his gaze. She noticed a mist of dust and sand approaching.

"Holy guacamole! What's that?"

"It seems there's a sandstorm heading our way." A violent wind whipped up. Then the sun faded, and a blanket of sand was upon them.

"Please stay calm. This will soon pass. We have an old

Egyptian saying: 'Nothing rests, everything moves; everything vibrates.'"

Pipper thought the saying must be true. Lumpy II was certainly vibrating. Maybe it was from the dates. Maybe it was from the coming storm. The sand moved quickly, overwhelming them.

Plans in Motion

While Pipper and Mr. Saluki cautiously made their way through the sandstorm, Hilda, Sophie, Archibald, Sidney, and Chance were in a storm of discussion at Pipper's house. Mitzi, Bull Bogus' head researcher, showed up as planned. She repeated what she had told Sidney earlier that afternoon and explained how threatening her boss could be.

"Is it really true that Bogus kicked his own brother out of the company?" Chance asked.

"My brother once gave me fleas, AND he listens to disco," Sidney confessed. "But, I'd still let him work for me. That is, if I had my own company."

"Mr. B didn't even let his brother take any biscuits on his way out," Mitzi added.

Sophie shook her head in amazement. "How come you still work for this guy?"

"When I first started working at Bogus Biscuits, I was in school. I was getting my food science degree and Bogus

Senior, Mr. B's dad, did so much for me. He taught me how to be a super sniffer. He showed me everything in the test kitchen and even helped pay for my schoolbooks. I was proud to be able to make healthy and tasty products. But now, Bogus Senior is retired in Florida, and his son, Bull, rejects all my formulas. He says they're too expensive. That's because they have real ingredients, not cheap chemical substitutes."

Chance was impressed by Mitzi's zest for healthy ingredients. Still, he tilted his head to one side and questioned, "But why are you talking to *us*?"

"I understand why you're confused. Even though Mr. B rejects all my formulas, he wants me on his staff because

I know a lot about the business. I believed things would go back to the way they were. If it weren't for Mr. B, I'd love to stay at the company. But he's changed everything so much, and this time he's gone too far. He's in a whole heap of trouble with his investors, and he's desperate. I'm afraid of how low he will stoop. Besides, your friend Pipper seems so nice. I would feel awful if something happened to her."

Hilda leaped out of her seat. "I have a plan. You can help us keep Pipper out of trouble, and we can help you get rid of Bogus."

Mitzi's ears wiggled back and forth. "How can I help?"

"First," Hilda advised, "you need to find out who Bogus hired and what his plans are for Pipper."

Archibald jumped in, "You said this punk is coming to meet Bogus tomorrow. I have the perfect devices you can use to track this creep. My Snooping Sound Sensor (the Triple S) listens through walls, and my Hide-a-Cam digital camera fits right in your paw. Batteries included." Mitzi perked up.

"Don't worry," Hilda assured her. "We'll be here to help you. We'll turn this Bogus into shredded newspaper to keep our Pipper safe."

Sophie agreed and advised Mitzi. "I'll be your contact. Here's my cell phone number. If I don't answer right away, I might have my nose in a book. But I'll call back as soon as I get your message."

"I'll do my best," Mitzi assured them all.

Chance put his paw on Sophie's shoulder. "You're always so calm. I know you'll keep Mitzi and me from shaking out of our fur. Maybe I should meditate more."

Hilda's tail swirled with excitement. "What an adventure! Mitzi, just give a holler if you need help with Bogus. We'll come running."

It was late by the time everyone left Pipper's house. One by one, everyone patted Mitzi on the back and wished her good luck. Then she left with Archibald to get his spy gear.

Next Day at the Bogus Biscuit Company

It was a new day, and Mitzi was heading into the test kitchen. On the way to her work area, she noticed a flat-faced character with spiky hair rushing through the hallway. He was muttering to himself, "Uh-oh, I forgot my watch. Where's my cell phone? Hmmm, it says ten thirty. I think I was supposed to be here at ten. At least I made it after dropping my briefcase in the street and repacking all my stuff." This rumpled runt was so busy talking to himself that he bumped right into Bull Bogus' office door. A voice barked from inside, "Come in. You're late (as usual)."

Mitzi pulled out the Triple S Listening Device and the Hide-a-Cam that Archibald had given her. She placed the listening device in her ear and wedged the digital camera between her front pads. Then she crept to the door and listened.

"Bumbles Brug at your service." She couldn't see Bumbles wipe his paw on his pants and extend it to greet Bogus. But Archibald's Triple S worked perfectly. She could hear every word they said.

"Bumbles, I have a new job for you." Bogus showed Bumbles a picture of Pipper from her blog. "I want you to follow this canine's trail. She is traveling in search of a secret ingredient. Follow her, and bring me back that ingredient."

"No problem."

"Good. She's headed to the Great Pyramid in Egypt. Here's your ticket and some traveling money."

Bumbles fumbled with the locks on his briefcase. He slipped the ticket inside and closed it quickly. Then he stuffed the money in his pocket.

"Any special instructions?" Bumbles asked, tapping on his briefcase.

"Just do a better job than you did last time," Bogus snapped. He eyed the briefcase curiously and asked, "What's in there?"

"Tools of my trade, sir," Bumbles replied.

Outside the door, Mitzi began chasing her tail in distress. "Oh, dear! Oh, dear! Oh, dear!" Then she phoned Sophie and repeated what she heard. As she was talking to Sophie, Bogus' office door began to open. Mitzi whispered she had to go and slipped behind a nearby plant.

"And remember," Bogus insisted to Bumbles, "do whatever you have to do to get me the secret ingredient."

"You got it," Bumbles replied and saluted. Then he closed the door behind him and walked away. Mitzi tried to get a photo, but with all her shaking, she only managed to get a shot of his paw holding the briefcase.

Mitzi sent the photo to Sophie. She apologized she wasn't able to get a better picture. It's really difficult to shake and shoot. She described Bumbles in his wrinkled trench coat with the dangling belt, his spiky hair standing on end, and his hurried way of walking (as if he were always late).

Sophie texted Pipper the picture of Bumbles' paw holding his briefcase. She sent along Mitzi's description of this curious character. Of course, Sophie had no idea Pipper was in a sandstorm with her phone turned off in the saddlebag on Lumpy II's back. She would have been blown away to know Pipper was being blown across the desert.

Sand Everywhere

Mr. Saluki had tied the camels together so they wouldn't lose each other. The sand whirled around them as they trudged on. The only thing Pipper could see was sand. It filled her ears, her nose, and her fur, even the creases between her toes. Nasty.

"I feel like a walking sand castle," Pipper sputtered, spitting sand from her mouth.

"My family is used to living with sand. In fact, my great-great-great-great-great (add one hundred more greats), grandfather was the first desert tour guide. He trekked through many sandstorms and saw many mirages."

"Mirages are like dreams when you're awake," Pipper reflected.

"That's right," Mr. Saluki agreed. "Mirages make you see something that's not really there. It's the sun's rays that do it. They bend in a funny way and make you think you see certain objects. My great-great-great-great-great (add one hundred more greats), grandfather insisted that one mirage he saw was real. He was guiding some of King Tut's cousins. They were bringing a mummy to be buried in one of the tombs. Suddenly, his camels refused to move forward. Just ahead of them was a row of dancing mummies wearing gold crowns. He was convinced the mummies were real since the camels watched them, too."

"Your stories make me think more about your relatives and less about this storm," Pipper commented. "Your family sure sounds cool."

Through the night and into the next day, Pipper and Mr. Saluki slowly crossed the desert. From time to time, when the sand became too thick, they stopped and covered themselves with the tarps that Mr. Saluki had brought along. As they made their way toward the pyramids, they shared stories about their friends and families. They finished the last bits of biscuits and emptied the flask of mint tea. Pipper was famished, but as the storm lessened, she suddenly brightened up.

"There's a tasty-looking kebab. Oh, some warm flat bread. Look over there! Watermelons!"

Mr. Saluki waved his paw in front of Pipper. "I'm sorry, Pipper, but it's a mirage."

"Well, this one looks good enough to eat. I can almost smell the garlic," Pipper said, sniffing the air.

Just as Pipper thought she couldn't go on without something to eat, the sandstorm ended. They found themselves approaching the Great Pyramid. Pipper's jaw dropped in amazement at the breathtaking structure.

"I told you not to worry. I knew we would eventually make our way here," Mr. Saluki said.

And imagine, he did it all without a GPS!

They parked Lumpy I and Lumpy II near Kepi's Kebab Stand and headed there for the lunch Mr. Saluki had promised. On the way to the counter, a strange-looking guy carrying a briefcase rushed past them. Pipper thought it was odd that someone would have a briefcase in the middle of the desert. That's like carrying your schoolbag to the beach. But, she was so hungry, she forgot about him as soon as they ordered.

Bumbles was so busy licking the last bits of his own kebab

from his face and dashing toward the Great Pyramid, he barely noticed Pipper and Mr. Saluki. However, he stopped in his tracks when he recognized Pipper's face from the picture Bogus had shown him. He sat on a nearby bench and hid behind a map he had of the pyramids. He planned to follow them once they left Kepi's.

Pipper and Mr. Saluki finished some spicy chicken kebabs and brought water and a leafy salad to the Lumpys. They walked right past Bumbles who was sitting on the bench. They didn't notice him looking at them through the holes he had made in his map. As they walked, Mr. Saluki talked on and on about the pharaohs. He told Pipper that when they died, their treasured belongings got buried with them in these mountain-like tombs. Bumbles could hear bits of their conversation as he followed them at a distance.

"So what do you think of our Great Pyramid?" Mr. Saluki asked with pride. "It would take more than one hundred Pippers standing on top of each other to reach the top. Isn't it an architectural wonder?"

"It's so big. Yet, it looks so simple with its sloping walls," Pipper observed. I knew Archibald would send me to the right place to learn about what makes the best design."

Bumbles wondered if design was the secret ingredient. He tried to hear everything they said. Mr. Saluki pointed out, "The Great Pyramid might be simple in design, but it wasn't simple to build. It took two million stones to construct this huge tomb. Some of them weigh more than thirty tons."

"That's more than Lumpy I and Lumpy II weigh together.

They are BIG, even for camels." Mr. Saluki laughed at Pipper's observation as they entered the pyramid. Bumbles thought Pipper was funny, too. Pipper and Mr. Saluki heard him chuckling and turned to see him cover his face with his briefcase. *What a strange fellow,* Pipper thought.

They continued walking and talking. Mr. Saluki led Pipper up and down narrow passageways. They walked through the Grand Gallery, a high-ceilinged hall in the pyramid. From there, they explored the Queen's Chamber and then, finally, the King's Chamber. It was originally made entirely of pink granite. The king's sarcophagus was there with its cover missing.

As they were leaving, Mr. Saluki mentioned that the cover and the mummy were never found. Pipper loved hearing about the mystery of the mummy, and she loved learning about the pyramid. She just wasn't sure it had anything to do with the secret ingredient.

Bumbles had been concentrating so hard in order to hear Mr. Saluki's story that he bumped his toe on the sarcophagus. He limped behind, trying to keep up.

When they returned outside, Mr. Saluki pointed to the pyramid's clean lines. He believed they contributed to its majestic beauty. Pipper figured that Archibald must have wanted her to see for herself that simplicity is what makes the best design.

Bumbles immediately texted Bogus to tell him the secret ingredient was the giant pyramid's shape. He was certain his client would be thrilled to learn all he had to do was to

make pyramid-shaped biscuits. Of course, Bumbles didn't realize his phone wouldn't work out in the desert. So, Bogus wouldn't get the message until later.

Pipper asked Mr. Saluki to take her picture in front of the Great Pyramid. When she looked at the photo, it looked like she was wearing a pyramid hat.

Pipper was impressed by what she saw. It was true the pyramid was one of the Wonders of the Ancient World. But, Mr. Saluki's story of how it got built was part of its wonder, too. Simple design must be important for a treat. But she considered, "Like the pyramid, there must be more to the perfect treat than its design. I guess I better continue on my journey. Could you please take me back to the airport?"

Uh-oh, Bumbles thought. I have to let Bogus know it's not the design after all. I'll send another text, and try to get to the airport ahead of them.

Bumbles took off his coat because of the heat. He fumbled with his phone and dropped his briefcase. Scissors, locks, and gloves tumbled onto the ground. Mr. Saluki and Pipper noticed him again as they passed. "What an odd guy," Mr. Saluki commented. Pipper added, "I thought he might be a mirage. He seemed so strange the first time I saw him."

Mr. Saluki laughed as he and Pipper walked back to the kebab stand where Lumpy I and Lumpy II were parked.

"Not again," moaned Mr. Saluki. Both Lumpy I and Lumpy II had parking tickets hanging by their necks. Pipper looked up and noticed a red sign above the camels. They were in a one-hour only parking zone.

Mr. Saluki and Pipper traveled back to the red tent. Pipper hugged Lumpy I and Lumpy II goodbye. She placed the crown trophy on Lumpy II's head.

"This really belongs to you," she told him. "All I did was hold on during that exciting race." Then Pipper got into the Jeep, and they drove to the airport.

Mr. Saluki walked Pipper inside the terminal. Bumbles was waiting behind a giant sign by the door. He heard Mr. Saluki wish Pipper good luck on her trip to Paris. She was going there to see Fifi Carniche who wrote a book about being healthy. It was her friend Chance's idea to visit Fifi in Paris, just like visiting Egypt and Mr. Saluki had been Archibald's suggestion.

Bumbles texted Bogus that he was off to Paris, to follow Pipper. Then he rushed off to buy his ticket.

Mr. Saluki wished Pipper well. "I hope this lady helps you discover the healthiest ingredient for the perfect treat. Enjoy the French food while you are there. Try the spinach quiche."

"I will. It was great to meet you, Mr. Saluki. You know so much. No wonder you are an Egyptian PhD (pyramid history dog). I enjoyed our trip and learned a lot."

"Come again. Next time, we will visit the other pyramids and the sphinx." As he waved goodbye, a pile of sand rained from his shirtsleeves.

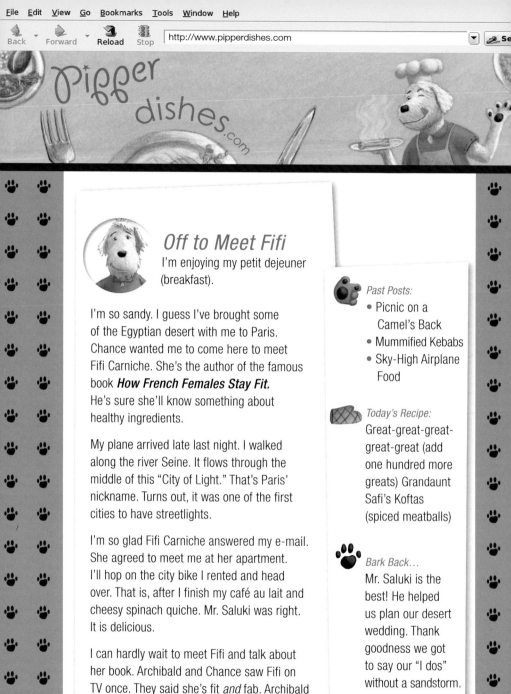

Off to Meet Fifi

I'm enjoying my petit dejeuner (breakfast).

I'm so sandy. I guess I've brought some of the Egyptian desert with me to Paris. Chance wanted me to come here to meet Fifi Carniche. She's the author of the famous book **How French Females Stay Fit.** He's sure she'll know something about healthy ingredients.

My plane arrived late last night. I walked along the river Seine. It flows through the middle of this "City of Light." That's Paris' nickname. Turns out, it was one of the first cities to have streetlights.

I'm so glad Fifi Carniche answered my e-mail. She agreed to meet me at her apartment. I'll hop on the city bike I rented and head over. That is, after I finish my café au lait and cheesy spinach quiche. Mr. Saluki was right. It is delicious.

I can hardly wait to meet Fifi and talk about her book. Archibald and Chance saw Fifi on TV once. They said she's fit *and* fab. Archibald thinks Fifi is trendy. Of course, Chance is more impressed with her muscle tone.

Past Posts:
- Picnic on a Camel's Back
- Mummified Kebabs
- Sky-High Airplane Food

Today's Recipe:
Great-great-great-great-great (add one hundred more greats) Grandaunt Safi's Koftas (spiced meatballs)

Bark Back…
Mr. Saluki is the best! He helped us plan our desert wedding. Thank goodness we got to say our "I dos" without a sandstorm.

Tina & Roy Doberman (Munich, Germany)

Through the Streets of Paris

Fifi opened the door to her elegant top-floor apartment overlooking Paris.

"*Bienvenue* (welcome), Pipper. It's so nice to meet you. This is Pascal. I told him you would be coming."

Fifi's rainbow-colored parrot, Pascal, kept chirping, "*Bienvenue* Pipper, *Bienvenue* Pipper. *Bienvenue* Pipper."

Pipper could hardly believe her eyes. She didn't know what to look at first – the bird, the walls covered with paintings and photographs, the huge windows with the striped drapes, the view of the Eiffel Tower, or the pink couch. Everything was just so… *ooh là là!*

Fifi practically had one paw out the door. "I look forward to showing you around Paris."

Pipper was surprised. She expected to just sit and chat with Fifi about her book and learn about healthy ingredients. She had no idea she would be going out into the city with her.

"That sounds terrific. I hope we can talk a bit about your book, too. I planned this trip so quickly that I didn't have a chance to pick up a copy. So forgive me, but I don't understand how French females stay fit. You probably go to the gym every day and don't eat any dessert." Pipper nibbled some Brie cheese and crackers that Fifi offered her.

"My dear, I don't go to a gym. And, what is life without dessert, or bread or cheese? I simply couldn't imagine. I am French. I am female. And I am fit. Spend the day with me. You'll see for yourself. Although, I must say, you look pretty fit, too. What do you say we head out? I have some errands to run."

Fifi threw her flowing orange polka-dot scarf around her neck and told Pascal "*à bientôt*." That meant she'd see him soon. She invited Pipper to ride on her bicycle built for two. Pipper left the gray city bike she had rented in front of the apartment house and settled on the back seat of Fifi's tandem.

"First, we must stop at the Sorbonne. That's the university where my friend, Professor Poumons, teaches. He is going to give a special talk about the opera *Aida*. I have to pick up a ticket for his presentation. I love the opera. It is so *dramatique*. Don't you think?"

Pipper nodded, "I read that *Aida* is about an Ethiopian princess who was captured and brought to Egypt in the time of the pharaohs. I never heard the music though. Mr. Saluki told me the opera had its first performance in Cairo."

"What a shame you can't come with me. I know you have to catch a train tonight to meet up with those circus dogs you told me about. So we will make the most of today."

Pipper was starting to think Fifi made the most of every day. Things were happening so fast. It seemed just minutes before she was having her quiche and café au lait. Now they were biking past Fifi's greengrocer as they approached one of the many bridges spanning the Seine.

"How are the turnips today, Armand?"

"*Magnifique,* Fifi."

"Please save some for me. And could we have a little bag of haricots verts? Just put them on my bill. *Merci beaucoup.*" Fifi shared the thin crunchy string beans with Pipper as they pedaled along.

Fifi's ballet teacher pirouetted past them on the bridge. They waved and continued biking.

While Pipper and Fifi were heading for the Sorbonne, Bumbles was listening at Fifi's door to check if anyone was there. He had arrived in Paris earlier while Pipper was lapping her café au lait. He remembered Pipper mentioning Fifi Carniche at the pyramids and looked up Fifi's address.

Once he was sure no one was home, he used his skeleton key to open the door. Bumbles tiptoed into Fifi's living room. He thought he might find a clue to where Fifi and Pipper might be.

"Who are you? Who are you?" Pascal demanded.

Bumbles hadn't noticed the bird and jumped in surprise.

"Who are *you*?" Bumbles blurted.

"Pascal. Pascal," the bird revealed.

"Where is Fifi? Where is Pipper?" Bumbles asked the parrot.

Pascal was silent. He just stared at Bumbles and flapped his colorful wings. Bumbles noticed the plate of Brie and crackers that Pipper hadn't finished. He helped himself to some cheese. Then he had an idea. He teased Pascal with a cracker, holding it near his beak. "Where is Fifi?" The bird started to grab for the cracker, but Bumbles held it out of reach. "First tell me where Fifi and Pipper went."

Pascal seemed to be thinking while he looked intently at the cracker.

"Come on now. Just tell me where they went. Then, you can have the cracker. In fact, you can have all the crackers."

Pascal couldn't resist. "Sorbonne. Sorbonne, monsieur."

"Thanks, Beaky."

"Pascal. Pascal," the bird corrected him. But Bumbles didn't hear him. He left quickly, relocking the door behind him. Pascal was alone again. He began nibbling up the crumbs in his cage.

Outside the apartment house, Bumbles hot-wired a motor-bike he found parked at the curb. He had no time for buses or metros or walking. He stuffed his briefcase into the bike's storage compartment, put on the helmet attached to the handlebars, and headed off. His map showed the way to the Sorbonne.

Bumbles didn't get far before a fly flew right in front of his goggles. It tickled his nose and distracted him. He rammed into a fire hydrant and came to a jolting stop. His briefcase tumbled out and onto the ground. Of course, it opened. All sorts of things fell out. There were his tools, a dress, a few wigs, and a tape measure. He repacked everything and headed off in a cloud of exhaust.

Just as he approached the Cour d'Honneur courtyard at the Sorbonne, he noticed Pipper and Fifi getting on a bicycle built for two. He waited in the shadows of the buildings and slowly followed them.

Fifi had gotten her ticket to Professor Poumons's talk. Then she told Pipper that she had to go to Madame du Whippet's perfumery for a new scent.

Madame du Whippet's was in a pretty part of the city called the Marais. On their way, Fifi and Pipper pedaled down a street and could see the beautiful gardens of the Tuilleries down the river. Bumbles wasn't far behind. Suddenly, they heard a voice.

"Fifi. Oh, Fifi."

"*Mon dieu*, it is Mimi. She is my hairdresser. That is her salon over there. She says my fur is so healthy because of my balanced diet. *Bonjour, Mimi.*"

Fifi suggested they stop for Pipper to have a shampoo to wash away the desert sand. Pipper agreed the idea was *magnifique*. Fifi's spunky energy was certainly contagious. A good kind of contagious, not like when you catch fleas

from a friend.

Meanwhile, Bumbles parked the motorbike and sprung into a public bathroom near Mimi's. He reappeared in a checkered dress and rhinestone sunglasses. He sprinted into Mimi's shop and sat down in the front. Someone offered him a complimentary nail clipping. Pipper and Fifi were seated in the back of the salon. Bumbles could hear them talking as his nails got cut and polished bright green – his favorite color.

Fifi and Mimi chatted away as Pipper's fur got washed and styled into a fluffy do. Pipper enjoyed Mimi's lavender tea. Mimi served it to all her customers while they waited for their hairs to dry.

Mimi offered Bumbles some tea, too. He helped himself to a few extra bags, dropping them in the pocket of his dress and smudging the polish on his newly painted nails.

Pipper's fur was finally dry. It was time to say goodbye to Mimi and continue on their way. "*Voilà*, Pipper, you look *très jolie* (very pretty)," Fifi enthused. "Let's stop for lunch to celebrate your *fantastique* 'do.'" Pipper thought Fifi didn't need much of an excuse for celebrating.

Pipper and Fifi stopped at a little bistro for lunch. Bumbles, still wearing the dress, watched them from a table nearby.

"I will order the *salade nicoise* with tuna, anchovies, hard-boiled eggs, olives and potatoes. It is the best dish at this bistro. But it is *énorme*. One salad is big enough for two."

They talked over lunch. Well, mostly Fifi talked. She told Pipper about her next book, **Why Frenchmen Look Good in Berets.**

Bumbles had also ordered the *salade nicoise*. He wrapped some of the anchovies in his napkin and stuffed them in his briefcase. He never ate them before and thought they might be the secret ingredient.

Pipper suddenly remembered to turn on her phone. She had been so busy between the sandstorm, the pyramid, the plane trip, and meeting Fifi, she forgot to check her messages. She discovered a bunch waiting for her. There was Sidney's warning about some guy who Bogus had put on her tail to steal the secret ingredient from her. *That's nothing to worry about*, she thought. *Besides, his scientists are working on their own formula.*

Think about it – she hadn't even found the secret ingredient yet. So there was nothing to steal.

While Fifi talked with the waiter, Pipper listened to Sophie's message. Sophie sounded concerned. She told Pipper all about the meeting with Mitzi. She mentioned Hilda's plan to work with Mitzi to protect Pipper and keep the secret ingredient from getting into Bogus' clutches. She even mentioned Archibald loaning Mitzi his Triple S Listening Device and Hide-a-Cam to spy on Bogus. Finally, Pipper saw the picture Mitzi took of Bumbles' paw and briefcase.

Geez, Pipper thought, *everyone seems really worked up over this. I guess I should be on the lookout for this guy. Though, I have no idea what he looks like. At least I can watch for that paw and briefcase. They do look a bit familiar. Hmmm.*

After paying the bistro bill, Pipper and Fifi got back on the bike and headed to the perfumery. Along the way, Fifi pointed out museums and metro stops. She took Pipper down narrow streets and wide boulevards. When they passed the Bibliothèque Nationale de l'Arsenal – a branch of the national library – Pipper asked if they could stop for a minute.

"I must take a picture for my friend Sophie. She's a librarian and, of course, she loves books. She'll be very impressed." Fifi also took a picture of Pipper in front of the

library. Pipper looked like she was wearing the roof of the Bibliothèque as a hat.

Finally, they arrived at Madame du Whippet's. "It will only take a few minutes to choose a perfume. I need a new scent to wear next month to the president's gala."

Just after they walked inside, they heard from behind them…"Ahhhhchooo." Fifi and Pipper turned to see the sneezing shopper. Pipper thought she recognized the checkered dress from Mimi's salon. She sniffed around the dress. There was a strange smell coming from this stranger. It certainly wasn't very perfumy. In fact, the smell reminded her of the fishy anchovies she didn't eat in her *salade nicoise*. She crinkled up her nose and moved away.

Every time Fifi tested a perfume, the stranger in the rhinestone glasses and checkered dress sneezed. Fifi was having a hard time deciding which perfume to choose. One smelled like peaches. Another smelled like vanilla. The third smelled like a pine forest. Madame du Whippet offered Fifi three small sample bottles to take home and a pouch of sugared rose petals.

"Come back next week when you decide, Fifi."

Madame du Whippet offered the customer in the checkered dress some tissues. She didn't notice this newcomer grab some sugared rose petals on the way out of the shop.

Bumbles stopped sneezing once he was back outside. He spied Fifi and Pipper sniffing the perfume samples while getting back on their bike. He scurried out of sight behind a

newsstand and quickly changed out of the dress. Then he hopped on the motorbike and took off after them as they pedaled down the street.

Fifi told Pipper they must go to La Charlotte, a heavenly bakery on the little island of Saint-Louis, in the middle of the Seine, in the middle of the city. On the way, she encouraged Pipper to taste one of Madame du Whippet's sugared rose petals. Pipper thought it had a curious flavor. She couldn't decide if she liked it or not.

They passed a beautiful carousel. Fifi insisted they stop and get on for a ride. Pipper sat on the painted camel. It reminded her of Lumpy II. Fifi, with her polka dot scarf flowing in the breeze, rode the zebra. The music played, and the city spun around them.

In fact, lots of things were spinning around. The city was spinning around Fifi and Pipper on the carousel. Bumbles' head was spinning around with plans to tell Bogus about all the ingredients he was collecting. And Mitzi was spinning around the test kitchen all worried.

A New Bogus Formula

One of the food scientists at Bogus Biscuits had come up with a formula for Boss Broccoli Biscuits. These newly created green treats were shaped like tiny broccoli trees. Of course, there wasn't any broccoli in them. It was cheaper to use green dye number 633-03-4. But this formula included way too much dye for anyone's good. Bogus loved them because he thought everyone would believe they were healthy. Mitzi was frantic. What could she do to keep these biscuits from going to market? Suddenly, she had an idea and rushed to Bogus' office.

"What brings you here, Mitzi? Excited about our new formula? We're ready to go into production and should have these green crunchies out to the public next week!"

"No, Mr. B, sir. I mean, sir... I think, she stammered. I'm convinced. In fact, I'm certain..."

"Spit it out, Mitzi. What do you want to say?"

"Well, I'm not sure they taste as good as they look, sir. What I mean is... I think we really need to test them with some customers. Just to be sure. After all, it would be a big blunder if these biscuits get out there and they don't sell well. The investors will be fuming mad."

"They're already fuming mad," Bogus howled. Why do you think we're rushing to get a new formula? They're on my back. But I suppose you're right. We could wait another few days before going into production. Get me some taste testers, and we'll test these Boss Broccoli Biscuits. But, don't go getting any chowhounds. They're too picky."

"Sir. I'm on it, sir."

Bogus was thinking if the taste test didn't work out, Bumbles was still on Pipper's tail and might discover the secret ingredient. All his bases were covered. So he thought.

Mitzi returned to the test kitchen. She had some time alone while everyone else was out at lunch. She phoned Sophie to tell her about the taste test. Sophie suggested Chance and Hilda participate in the test. They could reject this newest formula. That way, another bad Bogus Biscuit wouldn't be out there causing bellyaches. And Pipper would have more time to get this snooper off her scent before she discovered the secret ingredient.

Back in Paris

After the carousel ride, Pipper and Fifi continued on to La Charlotte. This was the tiniest bakery Pipper had ever seen. A large cake display took up most of the space. In the back, there were three small tables. They sat down and ordered the cake sampler. Little bite-sized pieces of La Charlotte's most popular cakes arrived on a glass cake stand. There were slivers of Charlotte Russe Torte and Ginger-Carrot Cake, a Lemon Chantilly Square, and a tiny Coconut Petit Four. Did you know that petit four means "small oven" in French? No wonder they are tiny.

Bumbles was drooling by the cake counter in front. He

was trying hard to hear Pipper talking at the table in the back. He heard her say she didn't have much time left in Paris. She was taking the Orient-Express train heading for Istanbul, Turkey. She was going to meet up with Boris Borzoi and the Flying Piroghis on the train. Then Bumbles heard her talking about the cakes.

" BOW WOW, Fifi, each little taste is better than the next. This carrot cake is one of the most mouthwatering goodies I have ever eaten. I never had one with ginger before."

"I suppose you know that ginger has many healthy benefits. It is especially good for getting rid of 'le gaz.' You know what I mean?" Fifi hinted.

"I do," Pipper replied. This cake would be just the thing after my friend Hilda's Five-Alarm Chili." Fifi continued gushing about ginger's goodness. She was most enthusiastic about its unique taste.

Bumbles slipped out the door to call Bogus from across the street. He was getting frustrated with all these ingredients Pipper was eating in Paris. When Bogus answered, Bumbles burst out with his predicament.

"I'm doing everything I can. The problem is Pipper is eating her way through Paris. I have a bagful of possible secret ingredients. There's lavender tea and sugared rose petals. I've learned all about how healthy ginger is. I even have the anchovies from the *salade nicoise*. Although, that salad has so many ingredients, it's impossible to know which one could be THE one. AND now she seems to be heading off to Istanbul."

"Slow down, Bumbles," Bull ordered. You're talking too

fast. Clearly, Pipper wouldn't continue her search if one of those ingredients was the secret ingredient. Just stay on the case. We may actually have created our own secret formula here. We're going to test it with some customers first. So, in the meantime, just do your job."

Bumbles had to hang up on Bogus because he saw Pipper and Fifi leaving the bakery. He hurried off to follow them. In his rush, he thought he had slipped his phone into his trench coat pocket. Instead, it dropped into a bush next to where he had been standing. He didn't notice and went on his way.

Bumbles followed Fifi and Pipper back to Fifi's place and parked the motorbike where he had found it. He was sure he had enough time to call Bogus back and explain why he had hung up so quickly. He reached in his coat pocket for his phone. Uh-oh! It wasn't there. He went back to the bike and looked in the compartment. No phone. He looked in his briefcase. No phone. Then he checked his watch and realized he had no time to go looking for it.

What a mess Bumbles had gotten himself into now. Bogus wouldn't be able to reach him, and he wouldn't be able to reach Bogus. Bumbles dove into a cab and considered his next steps as he headed for the station. He had to get his ticket and board the train before Pipper. And he had to figure out how to connect with Bogus.

Fifi was still going on about the cakes at La Charlotte when she and Pipper entered her apartment. "Here's a copy of my book. I wrote a little something in it for you. I enjoyed our time together. *Au revoir* (goodbye), *ma cherie*." Pipper thanked Fifi. She had to return the rented city bike and hurry to the train station.

After Pipper left, Fifi noticed all the cheese and crackers were gone from the plate she had put out for Pipper. She approached Pascal curiously. "Crackers *très agréable. Très agréable.*" Fifi smiled but then realized Pascal wouldn't have eaten the cheese too. And how did he get out of his cage? Very curious.

Just before Pipper got on her bike, she opened the book to see what Fifi had written. "Enjoy the rest of your travels. I hope you find your secret ingredient. *Bonne chance* (good luck), Fifi."

Pipper smiled. She was one pooped pooch after all the biking. Fifi, who was much older than Pipper, seemed like she could have done the trip all over again.

Pipper figured Fifi stayed fit by pedaling all around the place. She noticed Fifi didn't eat tons of food either. She nibbled a little of this and a little of that. Pipper enjoyed the delicious *salade nicoise* for lunch. She agreed ginger is a tasty and healthy ingredient. But she still didn't know what the healthiest secret ingredient could be for the perfect treat.

She did see a lot of Paris, though, and she got to know Fifi Carniche.

Now it was time to catch the Orient-Express train and meet up with Boris Borzoi and the Flying Piroghis as they had planned. Pipper was excited to see this sensational circus ringmaster and these astonishing acrobats. Hilda had hounded her to meet them. She said they are the most thrilling act since that magician, Houndini. Hilda was convinced these famous circus performers could help Pipper discover the thrilling secret to a perfect treat.

It started to rain as Pipper biked along. Her "do" became an "un-do." *Quelle domage* (what a pity)!

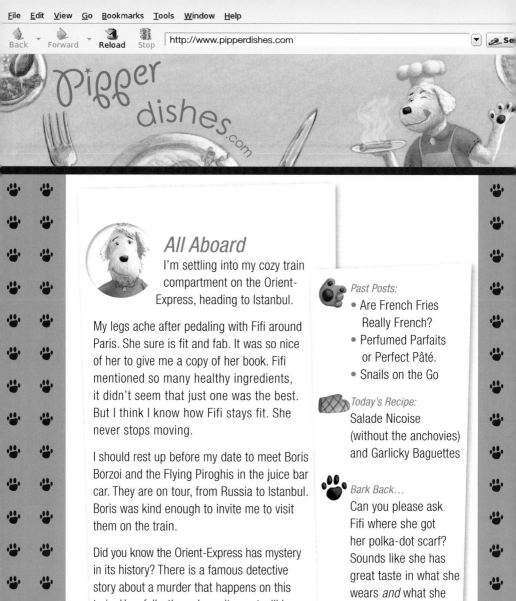

All Aboard

I'm settling into my cozy train compartment on the Orient-Express, heading to Istanbul.

My legs ache after pedaling with Fifi around Paris. She sure is fit and fab. It was so nice of her to give me a copy of her book. Fifi mentioned so many healthy ingredients, it didn't seem that just one was the best. But I think I know how Fifi stays fit. She never stops moving.

I should rest up before my date to meet Boris Borzoi and the Flying Piroghis in the juice bar car. They are on tour, from Russia to Istanbul. Boris was kind enough to invite me to visit them on the train.

Did you know the Orient-Express has mystery in its history? There is a famous detective story about a murder that happens on this train. Hopefully, the only excitement will be the Flying Piroghis and their spine-tingling acrobatics.

Past Posts:
- Are French Fries Really French?
- Perfumed Parfaits or Perfect Pâté.
- Snails on the Go

Today's Recipe:
Salade Nicoise (without the anchovies) and Garlicky Baguettes

Bark Back…
Can you please ask Fifi where she got her polka-dot scarf? Sounds like she has great taste in what she wears *and* what she eats!

Isadora Dachshund
(Liverpool, England)

On the Orient-Express

Pipper settled into her compartment on this famous train. She relaxed on the richly upholstered seat and looked out the window at the scenery passing by. She admired the wood-carved ceiling as her tail brushed against the cool brass railing by the door. She felt like she was stepping back into another time. She imagined all the royalty, celebrities, and spies who probably traveled in this cozy space.

Pipper was lost in her thoughts when she realized it was almost time to meet Boris Borzoi. She washed up and combed her fur. She pulled out her phone and took another look at the photo Sophie had sent. The paw holding the old brown briefcase sure did look familiar. She considered this as she left her cabin and walked to the juice bar car. Pipper stepped inside and looked cautiously around.

What a scene! The train was filled with circus performers. One juggled oranges. Another rode a unicycle. Purple doves sat on the back of a pony that was wearing a red pointed hat. Pipper checked out each and every one until she was satisfied no one was carrying the briefcase from the photo. Then she sat down and waited for Boris Borzoi and the Flying Piroghis.

Pipper had no idea that Bumbles was sitting just a few bar stools away. How could she? He was wearing a yellow kimono and a big black wig. His briefcase was hidden under the kimono. He looked like just another circus performer.

Bumbles had devised a plan to buy some time until he could get to a phone to reconnect with Bogus. His scheme involved making Pipper take a *very* long nap. He'd already arranged for that to happen…or so he thought.

A bubbly bartender asked Pipper what she'd like to drink. "A Peach Fizzy please."

While the pooch poured the fizzy, Pipper looked down the bar and saw the performer in the yellow kimono. There was no way she could miss noticing the stranger's paw with its smudged green nails.

The circus is filled with interesting personalities, Pipper thought to herself.

Suddenly, the door to the juice bar flew open. The other performers cleared out of the juice bar, and a purple carpet unrolled down the aisle. The first Flying Piroghi somersaulted into the train car. The second followed with a triple back flip. The third cartwheeled behind them. Each performing Piroghi stopped just before hitting the baby grand piano by the bar.

They stood on their hind legs and pointed their front paws in the direction of the door. Boris Borzoi leaped through the entrance. He looked like he was flying. His reddish satin cape flowed behind him. "*Rada tebya videt!* (Nice to see you!). I wish you all a rousing good evening!"

Boris reached into his cape and pulled out a red Beety Borscht Biscuit and handed it to Pipper. Everyone in the juice bar clapped. Boris took a bow and sat down next to Pipper.

"How do you do, Pipper? I recognize you from the picture you sent with your email. I could do headstands when someone is so interested in my work. I may just let you in on a few thrilling secrets."

"That would be brilliant. Your entrance was a thrilling beginning."

"*Spaseebo*, (thank you). That one is as easy as *Pirog* (pie)."

One of the Piroghis quickly slipped between them and grabbed the only biscuit in a basket in front of Pipper. Bumbles' eyes widened. He started to fidget at the end of the bar. *That* biscuit was meant for Pipper.

"Have you been doing this a long time?" Pipper wondered.

"I've known I would join the circus ever since I was a pup. I love the smell of popcorn. I'm crazy about fearless feats. I'm a born announcer, too. At least, that's what my mom and dad told me. When I was only three, I announced the time and weather every morning for my family. I announced when dinner was ready, too. Also, I have to admit, I think the most thrilling thing of all is standing in the spotlight announcing thrilling acts!"

"When did you..."

"HELP! HELP!"

Pipper and Boris turned to see Simca and Sol Piroghi smacking Sergei Piroghi across his jowls.

"A minute ago, Sergei was somersaulting. Then suddenly, he just tipped over and fell sound asleep on the floor. We can't wake him up." They continued to smack his jowls and tug on his ears. He didn't stir – not even a twitch.

Boris ran over to help his friend. Pipper scampered behind him. Just as they reached Sergei, he let out a great big snore. The last bits of the biscuit he had eaten blew off his lips.

Boris shook him a few times. He looked suspiciously at the biscuit crumbs on the floor. Since no one could get Sergei to wake up, Boris hurried to the phone by the door and called the doctor. "Please come to the juice bar car fast. One of the Flying Piroghis has mysteriously fallen asleep, and we can't wake him. I think someone has poisoned him."

"Why would someone want to poison one of the Piroghis?" Pipper asked.

"We are the most thrilling circus act in the world. Someone is jealous. They have tried several times to stop us. Last time, they cut the rope during our Flying Doghouse routine. Luckily, we landed safely. That's because our doghouses are made of rubber to protect us from dangerous falls. Of course, we never fell before – or since – that frightening incident. So you see why we must catch this mad dog."

Pipper held the door open for the stranger dressed in the yellow kimono. He nodded at Pipper and rushed out. Oops! Pipper saw something drop from the kimono. She picked up the small bottle he dropped and headed after him.

"Wait! You dropped something."

The stranger ignored Pipper as he moved out of the juice car and into the gift car. He bumped into a whopping wolf-hound who was examining a crystal vase. It slipped from her grasp and flew through the air. Pipper rushed over and caught the vase in her right paw, just before it reached the floor. What a save! She returned the vase to the shopper and hurried after the stranger. Simca and Sol Piroghi followed her. They didn't know what Pipper was on to, but it seemed thrilling.

"Sir! Oh, sir! You dropped something," Pipper barked at the stranger in the kimono.

Bumbles saw Pipper chasing him, but he couldn't hear what she was saying. He slipped behind a clothes rack before Pipper reached him. The Piroghis were right behind, hot on Pipper's tail.

Pipper lost sight of the guy in the kimono, but she did notice someone wearing blue overalls and a clown nose stepping quickly ahead. He was about the same size as the stranger in the kimono. Pipper saw the corner of something brown and boxy peeking out of the top of his overalls.

"That's the briefcase from the picture," she gasped. Then she started putting the pieces together. "I knew that thing looked familiar. I saw that briefcase and that paw in Egypt. So that's the creep who was creeping behind me and Mr. Saluki in Giza. And those green nails. Didn't they belong to the sneezer in the checkered dress at Madame du Whippets? This must be Bull Bogus' bully. I'll take care of him."

Pipper took off after this shady character. The Piroghis took off behind Pipper.

They all entered the reading car. Bumbles knocked over a circus performer balancing books on her head. Simca bounded through the air to avoid the falling books. Then they all dashed through the music car. Sol pounced over the piano keys. Whew! No time to catch their breath.

Everyone sprinted into the dining car. Pipper passed the buffet table with its platters of pickled eggplant, vegetable dumplings, curried fish balls, and seaweed salad. She couldn't resist helping herself to one of the curried fish balls as she ran. The swiftly moving stranger now seemed to be wearing sunglasses, a red raincoat, and a hat. He slid along the black shiny floors and knocked over a serving cart filled with cakes and pies.

Plates flew through the air. A lemon meringue pie landed on Pipper's head. She paused to quickly lick some off of her nose. The Piroghis juggled the other desserts as they moved along.

"Hey, stop. I know who you are," Pipper howled at the stranger while removing the pie from her head.

They zipped through the observation car and entered the fitness car. Pipper ran under the balance beam. The Piroghis jumped easily and landed on the beam. They gracefully tip-toed across and dismounted. Someone on the dog run alerted the train police who rushed through the door to the fitness room, running behind the Piroghis. The acrobats continued running, springing, and jumping after Pipper. And Pipper kept pursuing the stranger who was then wearing a purple cape. Pipper could see his overalls peeking out.

She hesitated, turned to Sol and Simca, and revealed, "That mangy mutt has been following *me* ever since I left Fetchwood."

Bumbles arrived at the conductor's car. There was nowhere left to go but off the train. He panicked, looking this way and that. His briefcase dropped from his overalls. Of course, it opened. The checkered dress, the skeleton key, and a makeup bag fell on the floor. Bumbles saw Pipper headed his way. He threw on his trench coat and kicked the briefcase and all its contents into the corner. Then he opened the train door and slipped onto the ladder on the outside of the train. He hung on as the train slowed, heading toward the station.

A moment later, Pipper entered the conductor's car. Her paws were sweaty, and her legs ached more than when she rode Fifi's tandem bike. The Piroghis stopped behind Pipper. The railroad police stopped behind the Piroghis. Just then, Pipper looked down at the bottle in her paw and read the label, LONG DOZE:
Sleep like a bear in winter.

"This sleeping potion was meant for me," she told the acrobats. "I recognized that briefcase under the kimono under the overalls under the raincoat under the cape."

Boris Borzoi performed his flying leap entrance. This time

he was carrying the sleeping Sergei Piroghi with him. "Did you catch the scoundrel who snoozed our Piroghi?" he asked Pipper.

"No, we didn't," Pipper admitted. "But the sleeping potion wasn't meant for Sergei. It was meant for me. Now, I realize. Sergei took a biscuit from the basket that was right in front of me. It must have been put there by this dastardly dog. He was sent to follow me and take the secret ingredient once I discovered it. How is Sergei now?"

"The doctor said he'll wake up soon – in plenty of time for the show!" Boris assured everyone. "Will you be OK, Pipper?"

"Yes, thank you, Boris. I'll be fine."

"Well, Pipper, you sure have experienced something thrilling," Boris concluded. There's nothing like a good chase to get your blood flowing. This is our stop. You must join us for our next performance. The Piroghis can teach you one of their thrilling tricks from their Feats First act."

"Thanks, perhaps another time." Pipper said. "I have a plane to catch. I have to get to Katz's Delicatessen in New York for lunch tomorrow. Besides, I think I had enough thrill for a while. Good luck with your show."

Bumbles was listening from outside the train door. He figured out he needed to get to New York and as far away from the Piroghis as possible. He jumped from the train as it came to a stop.

On the station platform, the circus photographer took Pipper's picture with Boris and the Flying Piroghis in their famous triangle formation. Sergei had just awoken and couldn't believe what he had

missed. Sol and Simca Piroghi held him above their heads. In the picture, it looked like Pipper was wearing Sergei Piroghi like a hat.

"Do svidaniya (until we meet again)!" Boris hoped Pipper's search would soon reveal the thrilling ingredient. "Maybe Katz's Delicatessen will be the scene of your big discovery. Have the blintzes. They're almost as good as my grandmother's. And watch out for that no-good show stopper." Boris took a leap and turned to face Pipper. He magically pulled a Beety Borscht Biscuit from behind his ear and tossed it to her.

The police officer, who had picked up Bumbles' briefcase and contents, showed it to Pipper. Everyone held their noses when the wrapped anchovies rolled out along with the tools and Bumbles' disguises. "I recognize that dress. He was wearing it when he was following me in Paris. And that briefcase matches the one in the photo Sophie sent." Pipper took out her phone to show it to the railroad police. Pipper told them the story of this curious stranger and why he was following her. "I'm guessing he'll show up in New York too," Pipper fretted.

"No worries," one of the officers said. "We have plenty of evidence here to put this canine behind bars for a long time.

We'll put out an all pointer bulletin. You won't have to worry about him anymore."

"Thanks, Officer," Pipper said.

Relieved that this dangerous stranger might finally be off her tail, Pipper thought, *Hilda's right. The thrill in something certainly makes it memorable.*

But was that THE secret ingredient to a perfect treat? She wasn't sure. She decided her search must go on, just like the circus.

Pipper dishes.com

The Search Goes On

I'm on New York's number 6 subway, and boy is it jam-packed. So is this trip. I'm meeting so many interesting pooches. I'm going to so many places and learning so many things. Except I haven't yet put my paw on what will make the perfect treat. But, I still have a few more stops on this journey.

I miss my friends. I wish Sidney were going with me to interview M. C. Beagle, hit singer and host of the Howling Music Awards. Sidney knows so much about the hottest bands. I'm sure he could get Beagle to reveal something about prizewinning music beats. At least Beagle agreed to see me. He's been busy recording a new album, but he said he would have time to chew the fat over lunch at Katz's Delicatessen.

Katz's has been around for a long time. It's famous. Even Boris knows about it. That's because a Russian who settled in America more than one hundred years ago actually started this restaurant. Then again, everyone knows about Katz's — movie stars, presidents, and the New York Yankees.

I think I see a pickle in my future...

Past Posts:
- Brioche or Bagels
- Turkish Delights
- Dining-Car Eating

Today's Recipe:
Beety Borscht Biscuits

Bark Back…
Can't wait to learn your recipe for the perfect treat so we can get nibbling on it. We know you'll discover the secret ingredient. We're panting in expectation.

Harry and Henrietta Huskie
(Cold Foot, Alaska)

At Katz's Delicatessen in New York City

Pipper entered Katz's. The place was crowded. Waiters were rushing back and forth serving customers at the tables. Trays, piled with overstuffed sandwiches, went sailing by. The smells were electrifying. Pipper's nose sniffed in every direction. With such delicious aromas, yours would too.

The fur on the back of her neck stood up as she thought about Bogus' spy who had followed her from the desert in Egypt and who she chased through the train cars on the Orient-Express. She couldn't believe that he had actually tried to put her to sleep and wound up sending Sergei Piroghi to dreamland instead. She wondered what happened to this no do-gooder. Had he managed to get away? Did the police track him down? Could he have followed her here to New York? There were so many questions she couldn't answer. She looked around to see if he was lurking at Katz's counter or at one of the tables. Nope. She didn't spy the spy.

Once she was satisfied he wasn't there, she browsed the room searching for Beagle. At first, she didn't see him. Then she heard him laughing and talking about the menu. There was no mistaking that booming voice. She'd heard it when she watched the Howling Music Awards with Sidney. Pipper noticed that there was someone with Beagle as she headed over to his table.

"Hello Beagle. I'm Pipper. I'm so glad to see you in the flesh."

"Thanks for meeting me here. This is Jack Russell. You must know him and his band, The Wags. He's a five-time Howling Award Winner. We road dogs come to Katz's for lunch a lot. We jaw about business. Mostly, we're here for the food. I'm totally pumped about the corned beef with coleslaw on rye."

Jack greeted Pipper and laughed, "Everything on the menu gets you pumped, Beagle. What do *you* feel like eating, Pipper?"

The menu was huge. Pipper couldn't believe all the choices. Everything sounded .

"Pipper looks hungry. How about the brisket and some noodle kugel?" Jack suggested.

"Or do you want to try a pastrami sandwich on rye? It's mile-high," Beagle gushed.

"That sounds good. I'm sure I'd be happy with that," she agreed.

Pipper needed to get these guys to stop talking about food and start talking about musical hits.

Beagle objected. "No, no. I got it. How about a knockwurst nosh? You know, *City Dog Magazine* named Katz's knockwurst the best wurst in New York."

"I'll have the knockwurst. Really, that sounds perfect," Pipper chimed in quickly.

"I think we should mix it up a bit, like the Woofers and Tweeters," Beagle added. "What do you think, Jack?"

Jack agreed, "Let's go for it."

Jack and Beagle ordered lots of things from the menu. Finally, Pipper took advantage of the fact that the musicians had their mouths full and couldn't talk. She told them a bit about her trip and why she'd been traveling all over the place. She explained why she needed to learn what makes a song award-winning. It might help her figure out what would make a treat award-winning perfect.

"It's the words. What you say and how you say them is the most important," Beagle declared.

"That's Beagle's take, 'cause he's a singer. I play guitar. So, I think it's all about the sound," Jack insisted. "All I know is that when my band mates and I are putting together a new song, we just knuckle down and put our hearts and souls into it. It's like the world around us is out of focus. Our music is everything."

Beagle said he understood what Jack was saying. Then he suggested, "You could say that about a lot of other bands I know. And lots of them never won any awards."

Pipper jotted down a few things they said. Then she looked up and noticed a window full of smooshed noses and staring eyes. It was a crowd of fans gazing in at them. Beagle smiled and motioned them to come inside.

Pipper didn't notice Bumbles in his crumpled coat,

squeezed in with the crowd of fans. He entered with the group and snuck over to a nearby table. He opened the big menu, quickly made a lookout hole with the table knife, and vanished from view behind its pages.

Just the day before, Bumbles had rushed onto a tram at the train station in Istanbul. He had gotten lost and wound up at the wrong airport. Then he sped across the city to the other airport and caught the plane to New York. He knew Katz's Delicatessen was Pipper's next stop. What he didn't know was that the sleeping potion bottle had his paw prints all over it. He had no idea the police were now on his tail. He still hadn't connected with Bogus. He had no time to get a new phone. And now, his briefcase was gone, too. Luckily, his money and passport were in his pants pocket. He was desperate to discover the secret ingredient and finish this job. He hoped Katz's would prove to be Pipper's final stop and the scene of his success.

Bumbles started ordering everything he saw Pipper eating, including the knockwurst and potato latkes. Back in Fetchwood, Hilda and Chance were at the Bogus Biscuit Company ready to participate in the taste test there.

The Taste Test

Mitzi had warned Hilda and Chance that Bogus might pop into the test kitchen and recognize them from Pipper's blog. So they showed up in disguise. Chance wore a fake beard and a fedora. The hat's brim sat low over his eyes. The beard was big and itchy. Hilda's blue hoodie and leather gloves hid most of her spots.

"I almost didn't recognize you," Mitzi giggled as she let them into the building and hurried them through the hallways. They entered the test kitchen. There were a few other taste tasters already there. Each taste tester was directed to sit in a separate little cubicle facing a small window. The windows opened and closed so the lab workers could pass through the samples to be tasted.

Three biscuits were being tested, including the new Boss Broccoli Biscuit. There was a question sheet for each biscuit. The testers had to describe which flavors they recognized and rate the biscuit from one to ten. Ten was for the best taste.

When all the testers were settled in their cubicles, the windows opened. The first biscuits were passed through. Chance recognized his as the Boffo Banana Biscuit that gave Archibald a stomachache for a week. He muttered to himself, *There's no way these things are coming anywhere near my mouth.* He quickly hid the biscuit under his hat and filled in the questionnaire, rating it a "one" – the lowest. Hilda figured she'd give it a try. She took a small nibble, and then rated it a "two."

The little windows opened again, and the food scientists passed the second sample through. This one had some sort of herb flavor. Hilda wasn't sure what kind of herb. Of course, Mitzi had warned them that none of the ingredients were natural. So it was obviously some sort of fake herb. Now, Chance had two biscuits under his hat.

Hilda could hear sneezes and "ughs" of disapproval coming from the other cubicles. She hoped Chance was at least pretending to try everything, as he promised he would. Hilda then received the Boss Broccoli Biscuit and popped it in her mouth.

Tastes like cardboard, not broccoli. And it's chewier than an old leather collar, she thought. She rated it a "one."

When Chance's window opened with the broccoli sample, he blurted out, "I bet this green one glows in the dark." Then he looked up and came eye to eye with Bogus. The blustering Bull Bogus had switched places with the fellow who had been passing Chance his samples. Bogus had come to check on how things were going. He had to make sure these biscuits would pass the test.

Chance realized he had to actually taste this one. Bogus was right in front of him urging him to take a bite.

"Go on," Bogus ordered Chance, "eat the whole thing. This is our best biscuit ever. I'm sure you will agree."

Chance tried to keep the biscuit in his mouth and not swallow. He suddenly couldn't resist scratching his chin. The beard was so itchy. Bogus saw the beard move to the side. He thought he recognized that face. Chance tried to move the beard back into position. His paw accidentally hit the brim of his hat, which fell off. There were the other two biscuits sitting on his head.

"I know you. You're one of Pipper's friends." Bogus roared as he lunged at Chance.

Chance scooted away from Bogus, spitting out the Boss Broccoli Biscuit into a garbage can just outside the cubicle.

Hilda heard the commotion and rushed to follow Chance. Bogus chased after them. Mitzi nervously watched all the hubbub from her workstation. Chance and Hilda raced around counters lined with flasks of bubbling liquids. The other testers exited their cubicles. They headed for the door, leaving trails of crumbs from the biscuits hidden in their sleeves. Bogus demanded his workers block the exit, but they just froze.

Chance and Hilda also headed for the door. They passed refrigerators covered with charts and graphs. Bogus cut them off. His bulk blocked the way. They were forced to turn and slink under tables loaded with trays and containers of powders. They motioned to Mitzi to follow them as they crisscrossed the test kitchen. They zoomed past shelves of biscuits in all shapes and sizes and in colors that didn't match anything in the natural world. Finally, they outran Bogus. As they reached the door, they heard him bellow, "Mitzi, you're fired!"

All the participants burst out of the Bogus Biscuit Company door onto the street. Chance, Hilda, and Mitzi barreled out behind them. Hilda led Chance and Mitzi back to the firehouse. They were all panting, and their tongues were hanging out.

"Oh my goodness, Hilda, you're turning green," Chance panted.

"Funny," Hilda replied.

"No, he's telling the truth. You must have had a reaction to the food coloring," Mitzi explained.

"Now you'll glow in the dark," Chance teased.

"Don't worry. We've had that happen plenty of times before. It should be gone by tomorrow morning," Mitzi assured them.

They all laughed, which helped Mitzi begin to calm down. It was exciting to stop Bull Bogus in his scheming tracks. But then again, Mitzi was now out of work. Then they went to call Sophie and tell her what happened. They also wanted to help Mitzi decide what she should do next.

Back at the Bogus Biscuit Company, Bogus stormed into his office and shut the door. The taste test was ruined. Now he really needed Pipper's secret ingredient. But where was Bumbles? Bogus hadn't heard from him in days.

Meanwhile back at Katz's...

Beagle, Jack, and Pipper were surrounded by adoring fans and paparazzi with their cameras. Pens and paper were flying.

"Oh Jack, can I have your autograph?"

"Ooooh Beagle! Would you sign my paw? I will never wash it again."

Beagle and Jack signed some autographs. Someone even asked Pipper for her autograph.

"She's the new backup singer for Jack's band," one of the reporters screamed. Pipper couldn't imagine how he got that idea. There were so many bodies leaning over them that she didn't have a chance to set him straight. Then all the reporters started asking questions at the same time.

"When's your next album coming out, Jack?"

"Beagle, who do you think will win the Howling Music Award this year?"

"Where's your band playing next week, Jack?"

"What are you guys eating?"

"How about we invite you for a taste?" Beagle suggested.

Jack and Beagle started ordering knishes and bagels. They ordered potato and broccoli knishes; corned beef, pastrami, and salami sandwiches; and bagels with lox and cream cheese. They bought root beer and cream soda for everyone.

The frenzy of fans noshed on noshes and pitched question after question at Jack and Beagle. Between bites and slurps, they did their best to satisfy their fans' curiosities.

Little did Pipper know that while this was going on, Sidney was back home reading about her in *Rolling Bone*, the online music magazine.

There was Sidney sitting at his computer. He was scrolling down reading about Dobie Pincher's stolen guitar, new speakers, and the latest road stories from bands on tour. Suddenly, right in front of his eyes was a picture of Pipper with M.C. Beagle and Jack Russell. They were all holding pickles. Sidney read the caption: "M.C. Beagle and Jack Russell chow down at Katz's with Jack's new backup singer, Pipper."

"What?" Sidney gasped in amazement. He picked up his phone and dialed Hilda. "You won't believe what I just read. Pipper joined The Wags as a backup singer."

"You must be imagining things. Pipper would never join a band. That would be a pretty daring thing to do since she doesn't sing on key."

Hilda called Chance who couldn't believe it either. "What happened to Pipper's search for the secret ingredient? She couldn't possibly have given up on that."

Chance called Archibald who wondered, "Did Sidney say what Pipper was wearing? Did she look cool?"

Archibald called Sophie who said rather calmly, "I'm sure there's some good explanation for this. Just wait for Pipper's next blog, and we'll know what's up."

Back at Katz's, everyone was ordering dessert. Katz's famous New York Cheesecake arrived at the tables. Pipper realized that all Jack's fans had become Katz's fans too.

They were slobbering over salami instead of drooling about the latest hits. They were raving about latkes instead of rockers.

Pipper's tummy was full. But, as far as the secret ingredient went, her head was empty. She had no idea if there was one thing that made a song an award winner. Even Beagle and Jack couldn't say for sure. She'd had a totally tasty time, but realized she wasn't any closer to discovering the secret ingredient. She thanked Beagle and Jack and squeezed out of the crowd.

Suddenly, there were sirens. A team from the ICP burst through the doors. Just in case you're wondering, the ICP are the International Canine Police. Pipper looked up in time to notice Bumbles in his familiar rumpled trench coat heading for the restrooms. "There's the guy you want. He's over there."

Two agents nabbed Bumbles. They handcuffed him and announced, "We have the goods on you, buddy. You broke into Fifi Carniche's apartment  in Paris. You dosed one of the Flying Piroghis on the Orient-Express. You stole all kinds of food in Paris. Your paw prints were on everything – that plate of crackers in Fifi's apartment, the bottle of sleeping potion, and that funky old briefcase filled with food, odd tools, and costumes, You're coming with us to get booked and locked up."

Pipper quickly explained to everyone in Katz's what was going on. She made it short because she needed to get to her hotel, pack her backpack, and get to the airport to fly to Peru. That was going to be the final stop on her fabulous, but frustrating trip. She was going to the lost city of Machu Picchu to hear the wise teacher, the Dolly Lhasa Apso, give a talk. It was Sophie who thought the Dolly might help Pipper find the secret she was searching for. Pipper needed to get in touch with Sophie to let her know Bogus' spy was no longer in the picture. She had no more worries. Except that she still needed to find what she was searching for.

Just before Pipper left Katz's, she asked a waiter to take

her picture in front of the deli counter. In the photo, it looked like she had grown a salami on top of her head.

As Pipper walked out the door, she heard Beagle reading Katz's blessing: "Ess gesunt (Eat in good health)!" Then Beagle started to sing.

Get down to Katz's

On the double

You miss out, you're in trouble

No more kugel, no more knishes

Empty fridge, empty dishes

Get down to Katz's

It's downtown

Come enjoy, come on 'round

Good food cooking, let's all sing

Wear your kicks and some bling

http://www.pipperdishes.com

Along the Inca Trail to Machu Picchu

Katz's knockwursts were a real . I didn't think anyone could talk about food more than I do, but Jack Russell and M.C. Beagle could hardly talk about anything else. For a moment there, I imagined I was a famous rock star, too. I still have no idea what makes a song an award winner. Even M.C. and Jack couldn't agree on that.

This trip is FANtastic and frustrating. Everyone has given me their time and included me in what they were doing. But I still don't feel any closer to discovering the secret ingredient. It was Sophie who wondered if there might be something none of us considered. Maybe she is right. Maybe, it's not the design, the healthfulness, the thrill, or the award-winning taste.

Hopefully, the Dolly Lhasa Apso will help me with my search. Sophie said the Dolly encourages everyone she meets to learn the important things in life. She's my last chance on this trip to discover the secret ingredient. There's probably no chance to meet her, though. She'll be surrounded by the crowds coming to hear her speak. I hope I get close enough to see her.

My guide, Pisco, is leading the way to Machu Picchu. We've pitched our tents for the night. I can't wait to see this beautiful ancient city high in the mountains. Mostly, I hope I learn something from the Dolly's speech that will help me find what I'm looking for.

We wake up early to continue on the last stop of my journey. *Luego* (later)…

Past Posts:
- Knockout Knockwurst
- The Dish on Knish
- Deck the Halls with Matzo Balls

Today's Recipe:
Katz's Cheese Blintzes with Blueberries

Bark Back…
I just saw you on RollingBone.com. You know you can't sing on key, right?

Your pal, Sidney

Along the Inca Trail to Machu Picchu

"We've arrived in the cloud forest," Pisco announced.

"Oh, Pisco, the trees are amazing, all wrapped in vines," Pipper exclaimed. "They look like they are covered in ribbons. Check out all the butterflies."

"You are very alert," Pisco complimented Pipper. "The cloud forest is a mystical place."

"It sure seems that way to me," Pipper said as she looked down off the side of the mountain. "I can imagine a dragon flying through the clouds any minute."

"*Cuidadoso* (careful)!" Pisco cried suddenly. Pipper didn't have time to turn around before a giant condor swooped down. The bird landed on her backpack and quickly pulled out her cell phone with his beak. Then he took off.

"Hey, that huge bird just took my phone." Pipper yelled up to the condor, "It would be very nice if you would give me back my phone."

"*Por favor* (please), Señor Condor," Pisco pleaded, repeating Pipper's request. He shouted to the bird to let go of the phone. But the bird ignored them.

Pipper ran along the path, looking up at the condor. She thought to herself, *I sure have been running around a lot on this trip. I can't believe just when I finally got rid of Bogus' bumbling snoop I have this bird on my tail.*

The condor landed in a gnarled and wind-twisted queñua tree. The giant raptor waved Pipper's phone in the air while hopping from branch to branch. Other trekkers joined Pipper and looked up at the busy bird. Suddenly, he started pressing the buttons on the phone with his beak.

"Lucky for me I have no phone service on the trail," Pipper chuckled. "Who knows where that condor would call."

The group laughed along with Pipper.

But Pipper didn't realize that her phone was actually working. The bird had accidentally taken a picture of himself and sent it to Sidney. Poor Sidney couldn't figure out how this bird's face showed up on his phone from Pipper's number.

He called Hilda. Then Hilda called Chance who called Archibald who called Mitzi who called Sophie. Sophie remembered Pipper was trekking to Machu Picchu. But who was this bird, and what did he have to do with Pipper? Everyone was very curious. They decided Sophie should text back and ask, Pipp did u send ths pic? If ur not Pipper, wht r u doin with her phone? If yr Bull Bogus' no good goon wr on 2 u. Watch out!

When the message came through, Pipper's phone beeped to say a message was waiting. The sound startled the condor who dropped the phone from his beak. It traveled down through the trees. Pisco caught it and handed it to Pipper who put it back in her pack. She didn't notice the message.

Everyone applauded. Pipper thought the condor had decided to return it. She waved and yelled, *"Gracias* (thank you). It's so nice of you to return my phone."

"That was good of you to thank the condor. Although, I think he dropped your phone by accident." Pipper turned to see who was speaking to her in such a soft and approving voice. She couldn't believe her eyes.

"Wow! It's you, the Dolly Lhasa Apso," Pipper yipped. "I didn't expect to meet you. I was just coming to hear you speak. My name is Pipper."

"I am hiking to Machu Picchu with many others who are also coming for my talk," the Dolly Llasa Apso told her. "It is so beautiful here, don't you think? I am flattered that you have come. What do you hope to learn, Pipper?"

"I have been traveling all over in search of the secret ingredient to the perfect treat. But I'm not having any success," Pipper sighed. "I don't know if it's how it's designed or its healthfulness. Or it could be its thrill or its award-winning taste… or something else entirely."

"Or it might be something that you know but don't even realize you know," the Dolly advised Pipper.

"Oh, Dolly Lhasa Apso, this has been the hardest search and my most challenging trip ever."

"Please, call me Dolly. All my friends do." The Dolly extended her paw to Pipper. "I sense something led you to me earlier than planned."

Bogus Gets a Call

"Bogus, it's me, Bumbles. I have some news. It's not looking good, sir," Bumbles admitted.

"Where in the name of Rin Tin Tin are you?" Bogus hollered into the phone.

"Well, sir. You see, I lost my phone in Paris. And I had no time to get in touch with you another way because I had to follow Pipper onto the Orient-Express. Then I couldn't reach you on the Orient-Express because..."

"Yes, I know," Bogus said. "You lost your phone in Paris, you muddling mongrel."

"Right," Bumbles owned up. "So I tried to give Pipper a sleeping potion to slow her down until I could get new orders from you. But one of the Flying Piroghis...the Piroghis are a great act sir, you should really see them. Anyway, one of the Piroghis ate the biscuit with the potion in it by accident. Then I had to get out of there fast because Pipper was on to me even though I was wearing a cape, or maybe it was the kimono. I can't remember. Don't worry though, the doctor said the Flying Piroghi would wake up in time for the show."

"Flying Piroghis? Why were you wearing a kimono?" Bogus asked. "Oh, never mind. Get to the point you bumbling brug."

"Well, I managed to overhear Pipper say she was headed to Katz's Deli in New York," Bumbles told Bogus. That was just before I jumped off the train and got away. I left my

briefcase on the Orient-Express. I couldn't go back. I headed for the airport to follow Pipper. But I went to the wrong airport."

"And?"

"And... I finally made it to the right airport and flew to New York," Bumbles replied. "I ordered lots of food at Katz's. That's when a couple of guys from the ICP nabbed me. I didn't even get to taste that delicious pastrami on rye."

"Would you finally answer my question? Where in blazing dog houses are you?" Bogus demanded.

"In jail…"

"In jail! I'm at the end of my leash," Bogus growled. "The taste test failed. You failed. The ICP will connect all of this back to me. I have to get out of here."

"Bogus, what about me?" Bumbles pleaded.

"What about you? I don't know why I hired you in the first place. I should have known better than to trust you after last time. All you had to do was sneak that load of biscuits into my brother's garage. Then, we could have pinned him for stealing company goods and gotten him kicked out of the business on the first try."

"How was I supposed to know he had an attack cat? It had such big eyes. And those claws…"

"It was a house cat, you bumbler," Bogus grumbled. "You can stay right where you are." Then he slammed down the phone and paced around his office. A few moments later, he pressed the button on his intercom. "Ms. Windhound, get me a cab to the airport."

Bogus went to a picture of himself hanging on the wall. He pulled the frame away to reveal a safe. He opened it and proceeded to pack all of the safe's contents in a small bag. Then he slammed his office door and ran through the hallways. A trail of slobber flew beside him in the air. Disgusting! Once outside, he took a last look at the Bogus Biscuit Company and lunged into the waiting taxi.

Pipper and Dolly in Machu Picchu

Pipper and Pisco had invited Dolly to share their chicken empanadas. Dolly insisted on sharing the rice stuffed peppers she and her guide had brought along. They chatted away as they picnicked inside Dolly's tent.

As they munched their way through the meal, Pipper shared her thoughts with Dolly and Pisco. "I traveled to four different countries and met many interesting tail waggers. Unfortunately, I haven't learned anything about the secret ingredient I'm searching for."

"Are you sure about that?"

"Well, Dolly, I'm pretty sure. First I met Mr. Saluki in Egypt. He took me to the Great Pyramid. It surely is a wonder of design. But how it got built is also a wonder. In the end, the Great Pyramid didn't answer the question of the perfect ingredient. Then I met Fifi Carniche in Paris. We were supposed to talk about her book about keeping fit. We ended up traveling around Paris on her tandem bike and eating lots of healthy things, which was *magnifique*. But I couldn't for the life of me figure out which ingredient was better than the next. Then, I met Boris Borzoi and the Flying Piroghis. One of the Piroghis ate a Beety Borscht Biscuit with sleeping potion that was meant for me. That's another story. But, I chased after the rotten rascal with the sleeping potion. That was thrilling. But even thrilling didn't seem to be the answer to the perfect treat. Just before I came here, I met M.C. Beagle and Jack Russell at Katz's Delicatessen in New York City. We talked about food, food, and more food. Even they couldn't agree about what makes a song a winner, let alone a winner treat. And Beagle and Jack *are* award-winners!"

"I, too, have met different personalities on my journeys – Shepherds, Retrievers, even Boxers. Each one has taught me something," the Dolly confided. "I'm certain you learned more than you think. What do you know a lot about already?"

"I am a food writer and a cook. So I know a lot about food," Pipper explained. I love to cook for my friends. That is why I'm trying to find that special ingredient."

"Sounds to me like you need to get back in the kitchen."

"Gee, Dolly, you mean go home?" Pipper asked.

"Well, first you should finish this trek and come hear my talk. I think some of what I have to share may interest you," the Dolly said.

Pipper asked Pisco to take a photo of her in the cloud forest. Just before he pressed the camera button, the condor soared above Pipper's head and perched in a tree behind her. In the photo, it looked like the condor was sitting on

Pipper's head. What a silly sight!

Pipper, Pisco, the Dolly Lhasa Apso, and the other travelers tramped on for two more days. They passed through a high mountain desert and a jungle full of orchids. Pipper sniffed the bogglingly beautiful blooms. She and the other trekkers feasted on yucca root soup and juicy cherimoyas. The flavors were exotic and exciting, even for Pipper's sophisticated taste buds!

The travelers also stopped to enjoy hot spring baths near the ancient city. The bubbly waters tickled their undersides and relaxed their tired paws.

Finally, they reached Machu Picchu with its amazing ruins of long-ago palaces, temples, and dwellings. Pipper decided the ancient Incas who had lived on these steep slopes must have gotten lots of exercise going up and down.

The Dolly arranged for Pipper to have a special seat up front near where she spoke. During her talk, she discussed life's adventures. She said that everyone searches for meaning, happiness, and truth – even when they are making a treat.

She finished by advising the crowd, "You can travel far and wide, but usually you will find just what you're looking for in your own backyard... maybe even in your own kitchen."

The Dolly winked at Pipper when she said this. Pipper blushed and looked up at the beautiful sky. She noticed

the condor hovering on a ruin nearby. Perhaps he was
listening to the Dolly, too.

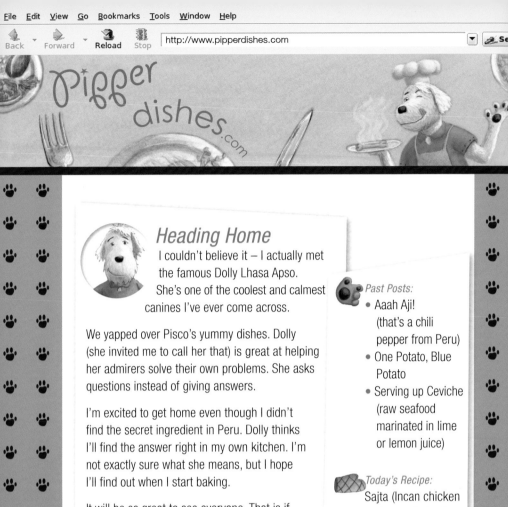

Heading Home

I couldn't believe it – I actually met the famous Dolly Lhasa Apso. She's one of the coolest and calmest canines I've ever come across.

We yapped over Pisco's yummy dishes. Dolly (she invited me to call her that) is great at helping her admirers solve their own problems. She asks questions instead of giving answers.

I'm excited to get home even though I didn't find the secret ingredient in Peru. Dolly thinks I'll find the answer right in my own kitchen. I'm not exactly sure what she means, but I hope I'll find out when I start baking.

It will be so great to see everyone. That is if this plane ever takes off. There's a storm. We have to sit here in the airport until it clears. Hmmm... I was so excited about being with Dolly, I haven't even looked at my phone. What do you know? There's a message here from Sophie who's wondering what happened to me. Let's just say a big bird stole my phone and took a picture of himself. That bird sure was talented.

Anyway, I'll be home tomorrow. My pals better roll up their sleeves. We're going to get cooking!

I'll keep you posted, Pipper.

Past Posts:
- Aaah Aji! (that's a chili pepper from Peru)
- One Potato, Blue Potato
- Serving up Ceviche (raw seafood marinated in lime or lemon juice)

Today's Recipe:
Sajta (Incan chicken and peanut stew)

Bark Back...
I read the Dolly's last book, ***Fill What's Empty, Empty What's Full, and Scratch Where It Itches.*** It changed my life. Hang in there, Pipper. You'll find your secret ingredient.

Berger Picard, (Gnaw Bone, Indiana)

Pipper's WonderBars

Pipper looked at the clouds out the plane window and considered all the places she'd been. So much had happened in such a short time. At least she was able to get a few souvenirs to bring back for her friends. She couldn't wait to see everyone and share her experiences. And she couldn't wait to start baking.

Just as she began to think about her travels, Pipper fell asleep. She dreamed she was rollerblading, carrying trays and trays of treats. She balanced the trays as she traveled over sandy desert dunes. Lumpy I and Lumpy II snorted hello as she moved past them.

Suddenly, she was in front of the carousel in Paris. Fifi waved as she pedaled by on her bike. Pipper turned with the gleaming trays, piled with treats.

Then Bumbles hurried past her in his rumpled trench coat. He was riding his briefcase like a skateboard. It had its own wheels. He lifted a few biscuits from one of her trays and disappeared from view.

Pipper turned in her seat and snored softly as she rolled on in her dream. Now, she was gliding through the train cars on the Orient-Express. Boris Borzoi and the Flying Piroghis helped themselves to biscuits as Pipper skated on.

Before she could say hello or goodbye to them, Pipper was in New York, whizzing past Katz's windows. She could see Beagle and Jack at their table with a heap of latkes and applesauce on the table in front of them. They were so busy eating and talking that they didn't notice her.

The trays of treats felt heavy, but Pipper rolled on. She was moving through the terraces of Machu Picchu. Out of the blue, the giant condor swept down and grabbed a treat. He smiled at her as he winged his way back up into the sky.

Pipper sure has interesting dreams. In this dream, she was very tired. She wanted to put the trays of biscuits down and rest.

"Be sure your trays and seats are in the upright position and your seatbelts are securely fastened. We will be landing in five minutes," the flight attendant announced. Pipper woke up and realized she'd been dreaming. She wasn't wearing skates, and there was no tray of treats.

Once the plane landed, she put on her backpack and headed out into the terminal. SURPRISE! Everyone was there to meet her – Sidney, Hilda, Archibald, Chance, and Sophie. Mitzi was there, too. She had been hanging out with Pipper's friends since Bogus fired her. She was so excited to finally get to meet Pipper. And Pipper, of course, was delighted to meet Mitzi. She thanked Mitzi for helping stop Bogus and his snoop, Bumbles, from ruining her trip.

Everybody was full of questions and news. Pipper could hardly catch her breath. She got so many welcoming hugs, she felt like a squeezed lemon.

They all piled into Sophie's station wagon and headed for Pipper's house.

Once they arrived, everyone gathered around Pipper in her living room. She eagerly unpacked the special souvenirs she had brought for them.

"You're so thoughtful, Pipper," Sidney said.

"I would never have taken this trip if it hadn't been for you guys. Besides, you know, I always try to bring you back little reminders of where I've been. It's a way to share my experiences with you."

"I hope you brought back lots of thrilling stories," Hilda said with anticipation.

"You can be sure of that." Pipper described the sandstorm and raved about Mr. Saluki being such a great tour guide. "He knows a lot of history. Luckily, he knew a lot about sandstorms, too!"

Pipper thanked Archibald for suggesting she visit the Great Pyramid of Giza. She told them all about its majestic, but simple beauty. She said she guessed Archibald always knew simplicity was the key to beautiful design. Then she gave him a piece of papyrus paper that Mr. Saluki sent along. It had Archibald's name spelled in Egyptian hieroglyphics. He was tickled by this thoughtful gift.

Chance unwrapped a box of crystallized ginger Pipper brought him from Paris. He thanked Pipper as he sniffed the spice to check if it was fresh. Pipper mentioned the healthy benefits listed on the package. "Fifi says ginger is good for her tummy and that she never suffers from *le gaz*. She eats some ginger every day. That is, after her classes and her shopping and before she goes to the opera or the theater or wherever. That Fifi never stops having fun. She has what the French call *joie de vivre* – a love of life."

"Here, Hilda," Pipper said, "I brought you a ticket to the circus and another ticket for a boat tour on the *Meteor*. It's a high-speed hydrofoil that travels from Saint Petersburg to Peterhof, which was the home of The Russian Tsar, Peter the Great. The Flying Piroghis will be performing in the park there surrounded by 144 fountains."

Pipper told Hilda, "I don't know what will be more thrilling for you – the boat ride or the circus with the Flying Piroghis."

Hilda blushed as red as her fire engine.

Pipper described the chase after Bumbles on the Orient-Express. She said she was really impressed by how much energy Boris and the Piroghis had.

She couldn't believe that right after the sleeping potion drama, when Sergei woke up, they still planned to go on with the show.

Sidney rolled over and yipped when Pipper gave him a New York City Metrocard and an invitation to the next Howling Music Awards. Everyone laughed at the story of M.C. Beagle and Jack Russell feasting at Katz's Delicatessen.

"I think that Beagle and Jack are as crazy about their fans as they are about their music (and as crazy as they are about Katz's)," Pipper joked.

Sophie had been enjoying listening to Pipper's stories and watching everyone get their special gifts. Finally, it was her turn. Pipper presented her with a signed preview copy of the Dolly Lhasa Apso's newest book, *Sniff, Look, and Listen*. "To Sophie, Pipper has told me so much about you. Especially how much you love to read. Perhaps I can learn something from you one day, too."

"My goodness, Pipper," Sophie marveled. "Leave it to you to actually meet the Dolly Lhasa Apso. I can't believe you asked her to write something to me! I'll treasure this book always."

Archibald wondered out loud, "How did you have time to get us souvenirs? You hardly had time to get from one place to the other."

"I'm amazed you didn't miss your planes or trains! I told you to give yourself more time on this trip," Chance reminded Pipper.

"I thought about that, Chance. I worried that if I only had spent more time in each place, I might have discovered the secret ingredient after all. But then, Dolly said I would probably find what I'm searching for right here."

"Yeah, right here in your own kitchen. What did she mean by that?"

"I guess we'll all find out, Sidney. Are you guys up to doing some baking? You, too, Mitzi."

"You must be tired," Sophie said. "We can't believe you want to cook today."

"Actually, I can't wait to get busy in the kitchen, Sophie. I seem to have extra energy after meeting Dolly."

Pipper gave everyone an apron. She even had a puppy-sized one that fit Mitzi perfectly. Then she went to her cupboard and her fridge. She took out carrots and parsley, tomatoes and grains. There was a bag of buckwheat and box of quinoa. "I think we should make these biscuits with quinoa. The Incas thought that quinoa was a divine plant. Pisco told me they called it the mother of all grains. This recipe is in honor of the Dolly Llasa Apso. She's the one who suggested I would find the secret ingredient here in this kitchen."

"Maybe it's the quinoa!" Chance suggested. "It's the best because it is totally nutritious." Mitzi agreed.

They set about measuring and mixing, slicing and dicing. Hilda worked on the broth that would get mixed into the biscuits. Sidney helped Pipper measure the quinoa, buckwheat, and flour. Chance chopped the vegetables. He was the most expert and careful with a knife. Mitzi suggested how much they would need of each ingredient. Archibald was busy digging through Pipper's biscuit cutters. He chose the bone-shaped ones. Then he reminded everyone, "I think a bone has a simple, clean design, just like the pyramids."

Everyone was laughing and chatting and busy baking. They mixed and rolled and cut the dough into bone-shaped biscuits. The first batch of biscuits went into the oven. When they came out, the second batch was already cut and ready to go in.

Once everything was out of the oven, Pipper and her friends took a break and piled in front of the TV to relax. Chance wanted to see the weather report. And they all wanted to know who won the soccer match between the Diggers and the Birders.

Mitzi flipped on the remote and settled down next to Sophie on her cushion. After the weather forecast and a commercial for flea control, a reporter interrupted with a major news update. "This just in. Bull Bogus, former president of the Bogus Biscuit Company who was responsible for its downfall, was taken into custody today. A former investor of the Bogus Biscuit Company spotted him on a small island in the Caribbean. Bogus was leading a group of tourists into the water to go snorkeling when the ICP grabbed him. The tourists in his group flipped in their flippers, watching him get pawcuffed."

"Well, he certainly got what was coming to him." Mitzi said, shaking with delight.

Chance agreed, "They must have arrested him for false advertising."

"I bet that Bumbles guy spilled the beans," Hilda guessed.

"He must have told the ICP that Bogus hired him. And

I'm sure he blamed Bogus for the sleeping potion incident on the Orient-Express."

Sidney said, "Well if you ask me, Bogus got his just desserts. Now it's time for us to get ours." Everyone laughed as they headed back to the cooling biscuits.

The kitchen was filled with wonderful smells and trays of treats. "It's time to test the biscuits everyone!" They started munching and munching. And munching. And humming.

"These are totally delicious."

"I'm with you, Sophie." Archibald agreed. "They look great, too, don't you think?"

"Right you are," Hilda replied. "I think they are thrilling to boot."

"Hey, Hilda, don't forget they are good for you," Chance and Mitzi agreed.

Everyone started speaking at the same time.

"We can't remember having so much fun, Pipper."

"We just love these biscuits."

"We loved making them."

"They're wonderful. Hey, we should call them 'Wonder-Bars!'"

Pipper's eyes lit up. She grinned from ear to ear. "I've got it!"

"Huh? What have you got, Pipp?" Sidney asked.

"I know the secret ingredient," she said with a grin.

Everyone stopped talking and looked at Pipper.

"It's love. You see, everyone I met on my search knew it all along. Mr. Saluki loves being a guide and helping visitors enjoy his land. Fifi loves everything she does. And she loves sharing the city she loves. Boris Borzoi and the Flying Piroghis love to perform and entertain. They truly flip to thrill a crowd. Beagle and Jack Russell love to please their fans with their music. And Dolly, well Dolly, loves to help people discover the love they have inside them."

"And, you, Pipper. What do you love?" Sidney asked.

"Well, I love all of you, and I love food. So, I guess my biggest love is cooking together."

Everyone was so excited to finally have discovered the secret ingredient. They kept talking about the wonders of WonderBars. Then Pipper had a BOW WOW idea.

"What do you think about opening a bakery and making treats?" she suggested to her friends. "I wonder if you could help me out." Everyone was delighted with the plan and promised to pitch in.

Pipper got ready for business. She bought extra pans, more

cookie cutters, rolling pins, and extra sponges for wiping up. She ordered giant sacks of grains and tomatoes by the bushel. She even grew her own parsley.

Sidney began delivering WonderBar order forms with the mail. Of course, he got the word out, chatting about Pipper's BOW WOW Bakery to everyone on his route. He worked at the bakery after he delivered the mail.

Hilda worked in the bakery on her days off. She also came after work, especially when there were no fires to put out – or cats to rescue.

Chance came over from the gym when he was done with classes. He said he had to make sure everyone in the kitchen was being careful with hot stuff and sharp knives – and that the recipes were healthy.

Sophie had been thinking about retiring from the library. She realized the bakery would be a perfect way to spend her extra time. That is, when she wasn't reading. Of course, she became Pipper's ingredient researcher. She read all about different herbs and other foods to use in the treat recipes.

Mitzi was now part of the bakery crew, too. Pipper insisted she be the BOW WOW's food scientist and help develop and test all the recipes. She advised which ingredients went well together and just how much of each to use.

Pipper's BOW WOW Bakery and WonderBars became an overnight sensation. In fact, there was so much business, the bakery needed more space. Pipper moved it to a little shop nearby. She hired extra bakers to help keep up with all the orders. The treats flew off the shelves. Chance introduced them at the gym's Pumping Paws Fitness Cafe. Hilda kept the biscuit jar in the firehouse filled with WonderBars. Sidney passed out samples with the mail.

Sophie brought bags of the treats to her book group at the library. Archibald designed a special sign that hung over the door that announced which biscuits were baking and when they would be ready.

Pipper got interviewed for the newspapers and was even on TV. She was on the radio and on the cover of *Bakers Best Magazine*. She never forgot to tell the story of how she discovered the secret ingredient.

Quinoa

NEW MINT WONDERBAR

While working in the prison library, Bogus saw the cover photo with Pipper's picture. There she was, holding up one of her popular WonderBars. There he was in his prison suit, sorting books and tidying up the magazine racks. Bogus flipped through and read Pipper's story. "Why, that furball found the secret ingredient after all. Now she has her own bakery, and the Bogus Biscuit Company is out of business. I should have listened to Mitzi and cooked up healthy treats instead of cooking up such a mess."

Bogus had a lot of time to think about the past during his prison days. Things would never be the same. But, he came to realize, they could be a lot better in the future.

Today, Pipper's bakery walls are covered with pictures. There is one of Mr. Saluki with one of his tour groups. Everyone in the picture is munching WonderBars. Lumpy I and Lumpy II are munching them, too. There is a picture of Fifi in her ballet class with all the ballerinas on their toes. Each one is holding a WonderBar. A snapshot of The Flying Piroghis shows them in one of their famous pyramid formations with Boris bowing before them. Of course, they are all holding WonderBars. In another picture, Beagle and Jack Russell are onstage. Each of them has an award in one paw and a WonderBar in the other.

In the center of all these pictures is one of Dolly. She is sitting cross-legged before

Baker's Best

• NUTRITIOUS FOODS
• RECIPES

PIPPER'S NEW WONDER BAR

a group. There is a WonderBar on a pillow in front of her. Pipper even hung up a letter and a picture from Bumbles. He wrote that he works in the prison laundry. He plans to give up spying and open his own costume and disguise shop when he gets out of jail. While folding all the guards' and prisoners' uniforms, he realized how much he likes costumes and disguises. He says he's certain business will be booming at Halloween. In the picture, he's holding a Wonderbar and waving at the camera.

Customers line up at Pipper's BOW WOW Bakery early in the morning. Some call in their orders. Chefs order WonderBars for their restaurants. Other customers place their orders online. Even Ferdie Magellan, the famous Portuguese water dog, ordered a ton to take on his sailing voyage around the world.

The kitchen walls in Pipper's BOW WOW Bakery are also filled with pictures of all her happy customers. Of course, the treats themselves are filled with love. But you already knew that!

Happy Birthday to Us!

Phew. . .I'm building up lots of muscles rolling thousands of treats every day. Chance is very impressed.

The Bakery is now a year old. Last week, we had a big birthday bash to celebrate. Archibald made WonderBar-shaped mobiles that he hung from the ceiling. Hilda brought a fire hydrant piñata filled with treats. The party didn't stop until after Fetchwood's mayor, Joe Cockerspaniel, showed up to give me the key to the city.

I hope you are enjoying my new blog. We post the latest poop about the bakery. Can you believe it? Senator Pointer was jogging by last week and stopped in for a bag of Dolly's Quinoa WonderBars. He read about them in *The Washington Boast*. Word sure is spreading about our goodies. Sidney took a picture of the senator pointing at me behind the counter.

Speaking of Sidney, you'll notice this blog also includes his music picks. Those are the ones we listen to while we bake. Of course, we don't always listen to rock. Last week, we heard **Aida**, the whole opera. Fifi sent the CD. She was sure we'd love it. When I heard the words about Egypt, I thought of Mr. Saluki. Of course, Fifi doesn't know Sidney is no opera fan. He couldn't wait until **Aida** was over so he could put on his favorite new band, the Cat Nappers and their CD, **Snooze**.

 Try our Take a Breather
Mint WonderBars (Mitzi's recipe)

It is great to have Mitzi on our team. She knows so much about healthy ingredients. You never have to wonder what's in our WonderBars. She and Sophie track down the best stuff to put into our biscuits. Be sure to check out today's recipe for our Take a Breather Mint WonderBars. They are refreshing and good for our breath.

Come back soon. You never know what, or who, is coming next.
Love, Pipper

Horray!
Mr. Doggerel bought our one millionth biscuit. We awarded him a free baker's dozen. He can't stop talking about it.

Sidney's Pick of the Day:
Fetch by the Runarounds

Bark Back...
Pipper, thank you for naming your Quinoa WonderBars after me. I hope I can live up to their reputation.

Peace, *Dolly*

Recipes

Just in case the story of my search for the secret ingredient got you hungry, I thought I'd share a few recipes with you.

I'm busy working on two cookbooks – one with lots more recipes from my travels, and the other is *The BOW WOW Bakery Book of Treats*.

Testing recipes takes a lot of time. First, Mitzi, Sophie, and I have to consider which ingredients to use, which go best with which, how much of each to include, how long to cook everything, whether everything is nutritious, whether Chance AND Sidney will both like it, what's in season and…

Attention! Attention!

Chance insists that before you get going in the kitchen, invite a grownup or older friend or relative to cook with you. It's important to have expert help with sharp knives and hot ovens. Chance always offers helpful safety tips.

Dolly's Quinoa and Buckwheat WonderBars

Archibald and Hilda have been eating these crunchy biscuits while lazing in the sun on the grass outside the  Bakery. Chance insisted they put sunblock on their noses before sitting outside. Mitzi told me that quinoa is considered a superfood because it has the most protein of any grain and is full of vitamins. It tastes sort of nutty, if it's not overcooked. Sophie read that In Quechua, the language spoken by the Inca, quinoa means "mother grain." I told you, Sophie knows about everything!

There's enough for everyone.

Makes 3 dozen medium-sized delicious and healthy treats for your favorite canine.

1 medium tomato, cut into large chunks
1 small bunch parsley with stems,
   coarsely chopped (about 1 cup)
1 cup cooked quinoa
2 cups buckwheat flour + extra for rolling
1 1/2 tablespoons sunflower oil
1 egg
1 egg white

Preheat oven to 350° F

1. Put the tomato and parsley in a saucepan. Add 1 cup water, cover, and boil. Reduce heat to medium, and continue cooking for ten minutes.
2. Remove from heat and cool. Using a fork, mash the tomato and parsley into the liquid. Drain the vegetables, and set the broth aside.
3. In the bowl of a KitchenAid mixer or food processor, combine ½ cup of broth and the remaining ingredients (except the egg white) until they form a ball.
4. On a floured surface with a floured rolling pin, roll the dough out to ¼ inch thickness.
5. Using a 2½" dog bone cookie cutter, cut your biscuits. Repeat until you use up the dough. (Archibald said if you don't have bone-shaped biscuit/cookie cutters like we use at the bakery, you can use any medium-sized shape you like.)
6. Place the cut biscuits, spaced a little apart on parchment-lined or greased baking sheets.
7. Using a pastry brush or the back of a spoon, thinly cover the tops of the biscuits with egg white.
8. Bake for 20 minutes. Remove from the oven, turn over, and bake for another 20 minutes or until slightly crisp.
9. Cool and air-dry overnight. Store in glass or crockery jar or paper bag (for up to 1 month).

Hint: 1 cup uncooked quinoa = 3 cups cooked quinoa

Buckwheat Is a Real BOW WOW

I was surprised to learn that buckwheat is a fruit seed related to rhubarb. It's got tons of fiber and other nutrients that are great for your body.

Salade Nicoise
(without the anchovies)
and Garlicky Baguettes

Every time I whip up this yummy salad, I think of Fifi and our lunch in the little bistro on the way to Madame du Whippet's perfumery. Then I laugh because I remember how Bumbles packed the anchovies in his briefcase and carried that smelly package wherever he went. I left the anchovies out of my recipe. I'm not a big fan of these strong-tasting little fish. Of course, you can add 4 to 8 anchovies if you want. This dish looks as good as it tastes.

Where did the anchovies go?

Serves 4

8   small roasted potatoes with the skin on
    (Chance says that's where all the nutrients hide out.) Cut them into quarters.
24 string beans, steamed or stir-fried until just soft with still a little crunch
    (Use Fifi's long, thin haricots verts if you can find them.)
4   hard-boiled eggs cut in quarters
16 cherry tomatoes cut in half

8   ounces tuna (canned, jarred, or fresh) If you're using fresh tuna,
    get some adult help in getting it seared for about 3 minutes on each side.
    Then cut it into thin slices. If you're using canned
    or jarred tuna, drain the oil or water first.
    Then break it up into bite-sized pieces.
16 black olives, Kalmata or whatever kind you prefer
    (pitted if you like – it makes them easier to eat)
5   cups mesclun greens or washed and dried Boston
    lettuce or any lettuce you like.

1. In a medium-sized bowl, put the tomatoes, potatoes, and string beans. Toss gently with ½ the vinaigrette. Set aside.
2. In a large bowl, toss the salad greens with the remaining vinaigrette.
3. On each plate, arrange some of the lettuce. Top with tuna chunks and olives. Arrange the potatoes, tomatoes, eggs and beans all around the lettuce.

Vinaigrette

This is a simple, delish salad dressing. Hilda is now using it in her Firehouse Salad.

- ½ cup olive oil
- 1 lemon, freshly squeezed
- 1 teaspoon Dijon mustard
- ½ teaspoon salt

Put all the ingredients in a bowl and whisk or mix rapidly with a fork. *Makes approximately ½ cup*

Garlicky Baguettes
Preheat oven to 350º F

- One fresh baguette, sliced in half, lengthwise
- 3 cloves garlic, skinned and cut in half
- ½ cup olive oil

1. Gently rub the bread with the garlic, or soak garlic in the olive oil and proceed to step two (2).
2. Brush with olive oil (use a pastry brush or the back of a spoon to spread).
3. Put on parchment-lined baking sheet and heat in oven for 6 minutes until a nice toasty crust forms. Slice and serve with the salad.

Hint: You can save time by making the potatoes, eggs, and beans early in the day or even the night before. Be sure to put them in the refrigerator until you're ready to put the salad together. If you do this, you'll be able to compose the salad in a snap!

An Unmixed Salad

Yep. Some salads don't get tossed. Their ingredients get arranged on the plate, and the dressing gets drizzled on top. These salads are called composed.

Fifi calls them *salade composée.*

At least there's one left for tomorrow!

Carrot-Ginger Muffins with Cream Cheese Icing

Chance loved the crystallized ginger I brought him from Paris. He insists on eating it as often as possible. So I try to include ginger in lots of recipes, both sweet *and* savory dishes. Savory is all the stuff that isn't sweet. Anyway, I always think about the Ginger-Carrot Cake that Fifi and I nibbled at La Charlotte. I decided to make up my own ginger-carrot batter and bake it into muffins. Muffins are fun to eat. They are really like individual cakes. The icing is a treat since it's got cream cheese and sugar in it. This not-too-sweet cake has whole wheat flour, walnuts, and carrots which are all nutritious ingredients, and of course ginger!

Makes 12 muffins

1½ cups all-purpose flour

½ cup whole wheat flour

2 tablespoons baking powder

1 teaspoon cinnamon

1 teaspoon ground ginger

¼ teaspoon salt

1 cup + 2 tablespoons sugar

½ cup + 2 tablespoons finely ground walnuts
     (If you or your friends are allergic to nuts, you can leave these
     out since the muffins also taste yummy without them.)

1 cup canola or safflower oil

2 cups finely ground carrots (approximately ¼ pound)

2 large eggs

1 teaspoon vanilla extract

3 tablespoons peeled and minced fresh ginger
     oil for greasing muffin tin

Preheat oven to 375° F

Using a pastry brush or paper towel, grease the muffin tin
with oil. You can also use a spray to grease the muffin pan.

1. In a small bowl, set aside 2 tablespoons of the ground nuts
2. In the bowl of a KitchenAid mixer or food processor, combine the
   dry ingredients (flours, baking soda, cinnamon, ginger, salt,
   sugar, walnuts) until well blended.
3. Add the remaining ingredients until thoroughly combined
   (oil, carrots, eggs, vanilla, fresh ginger).
4. Fill each muffin cup about 3/4 full with batter.
5. Bake in oven for 30 minutes until puffed and a toothpick tester
   comes out clean. Remove to a rack to cool.
6. Remove muffins from tin, and top with the cream cheese icing.
   Sprinkle nut mixture on top of icing.

Cream Cheese Icing
Makes 1 cup

8 ounces low fat cream cheese

1 cup confectioners' sugar

2 tablespoons milk

To the bowl of a small food processor, add all the ingredients
and process until smooth. (Sidney thinks it's always fun to lick the bowl.)

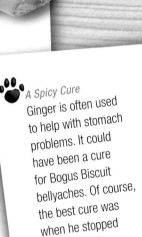

A Spicy Cure
Ginger is often used
to help with stomach
problems. It could
have been a cure
for Bogus Biscuit
bellyaches. Of course,
the best cure was
when he stopped
baking them!

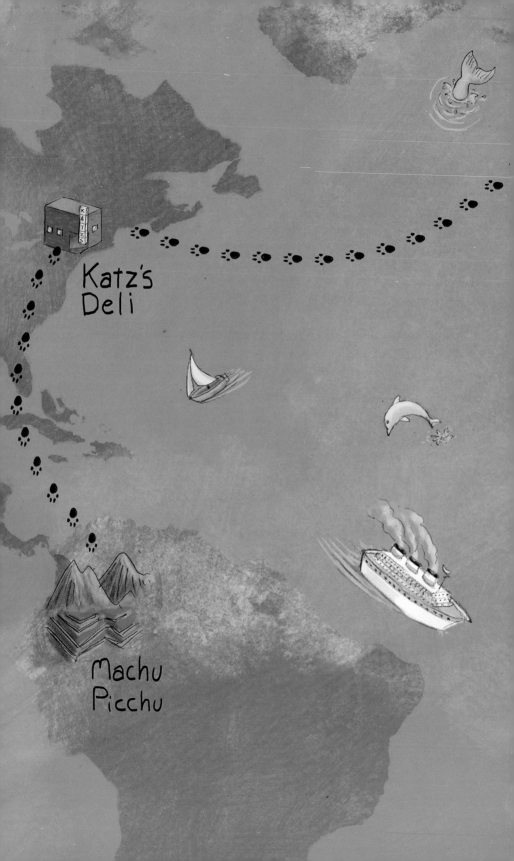